STONE AGE

BOOK 1

ML BANNER

STONE AGE

M.L. BANNER

ISBN: 978-0692026069 (Paperback)
ISBN: 978-1494556709 (Audio Book)
ASIN: B00JJPYTUO (eBook)
First Edition: 04/2014
Second Edition: 07/2014
Second Edition-Updated: 03/2015
Third Edition: 02/2017

STONE AGE is an original work of fiction.
The characters and dialogs are the products of this author's vivid
imagination. Any similarity to real persons, living, dead, or
undead, is purely coincidental and not intended by the author.
Most of the science and the historical incidents described in this
novel are based on reality, and so are its warnings.

Cover Art: Demonza
Editor: Karen Conlin

Published by

www.toesinthewaterpublishing.com

The Stone Age World

An apocalyptic solar storm takes the world into a new Stone Age
"A great apocalyptic story!"

Stone Age (Volume #1) – The Event caught all but a few by surprise

DESOLATION (Volume #2) – Survival is the only option during the new Stone Age

CICADA (Volume #3) – No safety in a post-apocalyptic world

REMNANTS (Volume #4) – Coming Soon

Stone Age Shorts

Short novels set in the Stone Age World

Max's Epoch –Find out what happens to Stone Age's favorite Character, Max Thompson
(Exclusively available @ www.mlbanner.com/free)

Time Slip – A scientist attempts to use a slip in time to save his wife, but ends up in a new Stone Age

Songs of a Dead Country – A survivalist fights to live and find his way in a new Stone Age

Want more about the Stone Age World?
www.StoneAgeSeries.com
Stone Age World facts vs. fiction; what's next; extra material not in the books; more

Thanks and Acknowledgments

To my wife, Lisa – Thank you for your strong encouragement, your creative flair, your support of my passion for writing, and your never-ending love; to my mother, Susan Banner – Thank you for your editing skills, ideas, and desire to help make this story the best it can be; to my friend, Patrick Carson – Thank you for your review, our discussions, and telling me to take my time; and to Dr. Jeffry Jahn -- Thank you for your support & constant friendship.

Finally, to you, my readers – Thank you for spending that one commodity which is irreplaceable (Time) to read this book!

September 2nd, 1859
Denver City, Western Kansas Territory

Russell Thompson knew he was about to die.

A fiery projectile from the heavens had hit only a few feet from where he stood. Churning earth and burning debris had lifted him up and over the camp, and discarded him into a pile of timber already ablaze. His mortal injuries and the flaming hell enveloping him worked at his consciousness. Before succumbing to the cruelness of his fate, Russell pushed back, willing himself to remember the euphoria of the providence that was supposed to have been his.

He was going to be rich and finally earn his father's respect. A tip from a dying man brought him here to a vein of gold and his destiny.

Then his destiny had changed.

He had been wakened this morning from blissful oblivion by the same unearthly forces still jarring him. It had started as a sparkle, what seemed like the early morning light bleeding through his little tent, in an urban encampment.

Maybe two hours past midnight, it was too early for sunlight. Yet prospectors were stirring in their tents, and outside, others were preparing their breakfasts and getting ready to stake their own claim in the mountains nearby.

Exiting the tent, he witnessed a sky beyond explanation. Red, green, and even blue snake-like tubes of sparkling light slithered in the sky above them. They were like gigantic, ghostly serpents suspended from unseen wires and moving in unnatural

1

ways. The light from these celestial beasts bathed everything below in an eerie shimmering luminescence, bright enough that it looked like the sun had already partially risen.

Then sparks and fire danced along the telegraph line, followed by the telegraph office exploding, and finally the Cherry Creek Saloon erupting into an inferno, launching flaming cannonball-like debris into the air.

A roar from the sky called him. He looked straight up and saw a reddish snake slithering out of the hellish nightmare above. It seemed to look right at him, just as his father had often looked at him, with anger and disappointment. His snake-father then started to shake and pulsate, looking now more like a giant dragon, who glared its scorn and hatred right at Russell. It grew before his eyes, swollen by all the years of angry words and disdain toward its son, hatred which could no longer be held back. The father-like dragon snake opened its mouth and erupted violence in the form of one of those fiery cannonballs. This one was reserved just for him.

Dreaded realization hit him. He was about to be consumed by flames. There was no running away from his punishment. He would not realize his destiny after all.

His eyes flickered open; he was aware he was moving, floating, his legs smoldering. With Russell's effort to focus, his vision cleared just enough for him to see that Pete, his best friend, mouthing words he couldn't hear or understand, was carrying him. Finally, unable to hold his eyes open any longer, Russell allowed the peace of unconsciousness to take him away.

"A Time Long Ago..."
The Valley of the Colo Tribe

A solitary figure sat on top of the only hill in the valley. From a distance, his outline, illuminated by the colorful evening light, was unmistakable against the smooth pile of stones on the bare hill that made up his rocky seat. Gord did what no member of the Colo tribe was allowed to do; he dared look up at the night sky. Doing this was not only against the rules, it was also an action that tempted retribution from the snake demons that owned the night.

No one was to ever gaze upon the eyes of a snake demon or they, and maybe their whole family, would be cursed with the Growth and surely die. Prolonged angering might bring its wrath upon the whole tribe. Were Gord not a visitor, he would have likely been cast out as punishment; it was a certain death in the harsh environment outside the tribe, with food and water in short supply.

The Colo tribe was not indifferent to his night gazing activities, but Gord was considered a traveler. Few travelers were alive anymore, but when one passed through, they were afforded a high standing among the tribe's elders. Their traditions, told through stories always beginning with "A time long ago," spoke of travelers. All travelers were considered wise, and some even had special powers. His father's father, Stepha, explained the origin of this could be traced to the original traveler who--before the mass death and the Growth and the colorful night skies--prophesied the coming of all of it. That traveler also foretold a day when another traveler would return and bring salvation to everyone. All tribes, like the Colo, watched for this prophesied traveler.

However, Gord had a job to do; he could not be concerned with their shortsighted superstitions. From his vista he could see the whole valley, lit by their so-called "snake demons." He searched methodically, unmoving, looking for some glimpse of the map he had memorized. Then he shifted his examination the measure of one hand-length to his left and searched more, analyzing what he saw. Like the rising and setting sun, his head followed a similar track slowly from one side to the other, carefully surveying every part of his surroundings with an eye toward the mountains.

There it was! The unmistakable three-pointed mountaintop as far off as his eyes could focus. He quickly jerked his head to the left and then the right, making sure no one could see what he did next. He turned his attention on the folded leather hide in his lap. Gently he drew open each end of the protective cover. When all four ends were unfolded, he examined with reverence what it held: a clamshell object with flat sides and wisdom within. Opening it up and examining its contents, he looked again at the three pointed peak before him, now with more familiarity.

A slight smile formed on his lips. He had found the clue that would lead him to Cicada.

SOMETIME
IN OUR VERY
NEAR FUTURE

To: Maxwell Thompson

From: bulletins@CMEResearchInstitute.org

Subject: Increased CME Activity Expected

CME Research Institute
www.CMEResearchInstitute.org

BULLETIN
25 June

With significant sunspot activity at the peak of an eleven-year cycle, we expect substantial coronal mass ejection (CME) activity from the sun over the next few days.

Using observed and analyzed data from SDO, Hubble, ISS, and other satellites, a solar proton event (SPE) was recorded measuring 100MeV, followed by two large CMEs. We estimate roughly 4% of the released magnetic fields and plasma will make contact with Earth's geomagnetic fields in approximately 10 hours. In addition to satellite disruptions and some minor ground-based electrical disruptions around the poles, there will be above normal aurora activity in both the northern and southern hemispheres, especially over Asia.

For more information go to www.CMEResearchInstitute.org and click on "Bulletins."

1.
The Kings
June 25th
O'Hare Airport

Four days before the world they knew ended, Bill and Lisa King boarded a plane to Tucson, where they planned to meet their adult daughter Sally and then drive to their family's beach house in Rocky Point, Mexico for a ten-day vacation. Initially, there would just be the three of them. Four days later, their two youngest-- Darla, who was twenty-one, and Danny, who was ten--would fly all the way, joining the whole family on the beach. Since Sally had left for college and then gone to work in Tucson, the Kings had not vacationed as a family. It was no easy task, as Lisa had been planning this vacation for what seemed like the better part of a year. After last July fourth, when everyone complained due to a jumble of excuses that the family never got together, Lisa put her foot down and said there would be no further discussion. They were getting together on the beach. Ever since all had agreed to "the trip," Lisa had been giddy with excitement, often starting out the family phone conversations with "You wanna talk about our trip?"

Bill was different. He had been more dispassionate about their trip until last week when a reminder on his phone's calendar sang out with its announcing horn, reminding him *the trip* was almost here. At that moment, he realized for the first time in almost a year he would not be working 70-hour weeks, staring at two monitors and occupying his thoughts with all the worries his growing business required. Instead, he would be reading an ebook on his Kindle, drinking margaritas, lounging by their pool or simply slipping his *"toes in the water, ass in the sand,"* as the Zach Brown song emoted. Mostly, he would be enjoying his wife and family in a few short days.

That day was today.

They were the second couple to pre-board their flight, and thanks to Bill's using their rewards card for his Internet-based business they were flying first class all the way. There was the negative of having to take the later flight. However, in a way, it was his preference, as they would be driving through Mexico at night, when there were fewer drivers on the roads and the Mexican agricultural inspectors and local police were at home asleep, meaning almost no chance of their being stopped at the border or in the border town. In other words, smooth traveling all the way to the beach.

"Good afternoon, welcome aboard," greeted a flight attendant while hanging up the first passenger's sports coat.

After they cleared the doorway and turned left, another Disneyland-happy flight attendant greeted them. "Good afternoon. Can I help you find your seats?" she asked warmly, and just genuinely enough to be believable.

"Those are ours," Lisa said from behind, thrusting out her arm with two fingers pointing to 3C and 3D, two aisle seats.

"Yes, ah, Mr. and Mrs. King?" The flight attendant looked up for confirmation in their faces. "What would you like to drink?"

Bill felt a buzzing from his pocket. Resting his bag on his seat, he pulled the phone from his jeans pocket. "Hi, Dar. Your mom and I just boarded the plane. Did you pick up Danny from camp?" He cradled the phone between his shoulder and ear and listened. "Okay . . ." He plopped onto the arm of his seat, knees in the aisle, shoulders slumping, deflating as he listened. "Not again."

"What's wrong? Did he have an asthma attack?" Lisa whispered frantically.

He shook his head *no*, briefly glancing across the aisle to her, and then looking down. "Good. That damned Johnson kid is going to get his butt handed to him by one of his many victims someday." His shoulders straightened more. "Thanks. You're a wonderful daughter."

The flight attendant now looked more Six Flags than Disneyland, awaiting their drink order, while Lisa tried to garner details about their son from the one-sided conversation. Another couple, wanting to get by them to the second row, grumbled their displeasure. All of them glared at Bill.

To the flight attendant, Lisa held out two fingers and mouthed, "Two champagnes, please."

"Do you want to quickly talk to your mom?" Bill stared at Lisa with an expectant smile. He abruptly looked up, just realizing he was obstructing the lane. "I am so sorry."

The other couple pushed passed him with murmured sarcastic thanks, trying to get away from the family conference convened in the aisle.

"Okay . . . please tell Danny we're proud of him and we'll call when we arrive in a few hours." Covering the phone with his right hand, he explained to his wife, "Dar just arrived at her class and can't talk. They're waiting for her, so say a quick bye."

Lisa nodded and craned toward the phone as Bill held it to her ear. "We love you, Dar. Thanks for taking care of everything. Kisses to you and Danny," she said in a louder voice.

"Okay, we'll talk some more later, love you." He ended the call.

"Danny stood up for two friends who were being bullied by that delinquent Johnson, who didn't like it and took a swing at him."

Lisa gasped, hand to her lips. "Oh, my. He's all right, isn't _"

"Yes," Bill cut her off. "It was just a little bruise on his cheek. One of the counselors saw the whole thing and stopped it immediately. Johnson is permanently banned from camp, although camp is over. Anyway, our little man is home now playing X-Box, while Darla is, of course, at her class. Well, you heard that part. His asthma is fine, too. Oh, and Dar wanted to remind us that they're driving to Mom and Dad's tonight to take in some of the lake activities. Guess your penchant for the water rubbed off on her." How funny, he thought, that Sally ran down to their beach house in Mexico all the time, they lived off Lake Michigan with Danny begging to go to the beach, and Darla, when on breaks from college, visited his parents in Michigan at their lake house every chance she gets.

"I told you we should have all come down together," she said, only half kidding.

After settling into their seats and sipping on their champagnes, Bill admired his wife as she pulled a pair of slippers from her carry-on swapping them with her walking shoes. She was a beautiful fifty. Still a natural brunette who kept her hair short for its utility, she now seemed to give off an extra measure of radiance, maybe reflecting the peace she felt starting their vacation. As always, her eyes drew his gaze, just as they had when he first met her thirty years ago. A barometer to her personality, they were often mysterious, always thoughtful and discerning, and yet frequently playful. When her face exploded in a smile, her eyes would sparkle like a July fourth finale. Those same eyes now returned his gaze. First, she acted puzzled, then self-conscious, reflexively straightening her shirt, and then smiling, realizing her husband's gaze was a compliment. *There's that sparkle,* he thought.

She resumed her routine, grabbing a Sudoku book and a pen, and two little black bags. Sitting down, she handed one to Bill. "What's this?" he asked.

"A surprise for later. What are our movie choices?"

He studied their inflight magazine for a few moments, then selected one. "*One Second After*, it's about the American power grid going down after a terrorist's exploded nuclear device generates an EMP."

"How uplifting," she deadpanned. Now her eyes and smile reflected her playful side.

2.

Steve Parkington
4:30 P.M.
Clear Lake, Michigan

Steve Parkington was up to the twelfth level of Killer Zombie Apocalypse Part XII on the X-Box when an unfamiliar tone from his computer prompted him to stop. Just before a Nazi zombie was to take a bite out of him, he hit the pause button on his controller and examined the smallest of the five computer screens to the right of his primary screen. His search algorithm had been scanning the 'net for specific keywords, and it scored a hit. He clicked on the link on his screen. This took him to an unfamiliar message board page. The page contained a simple text message of stark white letters against a solid black background and an image at the bottom. It said:

> Hello again. Our search for intelligent individuals now continues.
> The first clue is hidden within this image.
> Find it, and it will lead you on the road to finding us. We look forward to meeting the few that will make it all the way through.
> Good luck.
> 3301

Below the text was this image:

"Ha. There you are Mr. Cicada," he exclaimed excitedly.

He'd heard about Cicada 3301 from an IRC group where he often communicated with fellow hacker-friends. Most were twenty-somethings like him. By the time he had tried to follow the trail, it had grown cold. He'd written the algorithm to scour the Internet in hopes that it would appear again. His efforts had just paid off.

Arguably, his interest in this was due to a gene passed down to him by his father, John, who had founded two successful Internet-based companies; the second, called Picshare, had made his family wealthy. Steve, like his father, was an IT person by vocation, founding his own digital security company prior to beginning high school. However, his skills for this test were spawned by his long-time passion for hacking and cryptography.

"Okay, what is hidden in this image then?" he asked out loud, considering his next move in this chess game. It must use some form of digital steganography, the concealing of secret information within a digital file. He started picking apart the pixels using a favorite open source program. He ran different combinations, adjusting the color of every first pixel, then every second, and so on. On the fiftieth pixel combination, the image changed to reveal writing. There was a reference to "Tiberius Claudius Caesar" and a line of seemingly meaningless letters. He deduced it must be a Caesar cipher, an encryption technique used for private correspondence by its namesake, Julius. He also knew this as a shift cipher, one of the most widely known encryption techniques, consisting of substituting or "shifting" letters in a message with corresponding letters some number of positions down the alphabet. Since Tiberius Claudius was the fourth Caesar in Rome, Steve reasoned that for every letter in the meaningless jumble of letters he would substitute a letter four positions forward. This gave him a web address, which he entered into his browser, excited to see what it would reveal.

"Nuts," he said, disappointed. It was a picture of a duck with the following text:

Whoops.

Just a decoy this way. Looks like you can't guess how to get the message out.

"Okay, you don't fool me that easily. I'm guessing your duck message is a literal clue." Steve continued his one-sided conversation with the screen's author.

He opened his trusted OutGuess program, which had helped him in cracking many similar encryption codes. With that, he found another hidden message, which linked him to a message board on Reddit:

-----BEGIN PGP SIGNED MESSAGE-----
Hash: SHA1
Welcome again.

Here is a book code. To find the book, break this riddle:

A book whose study is forbidden
Once dictated to a beast;
To be read once and then destroyed
Or you shall have no peace.

I:1:6; I:2:15; I:3:26; I:5:4; I:6:15; I:10:26:; I:14:136;
I:15:68; I:16:42; I:18:17; I:19:14; I:20:58; I:21:10;
I:22:8; I:23:6; I:25:17; I:26:33; I:27:30; I:46:32;
I:47:53; I:49:209; I:50:10; I:51:115; I:52:39; I:53:4;
I:62:43; I:63:8; III:19:84; III:20:10; III:21:11; ;
III:22:3; III:23:58; 5; I:1:3; I:2:15; I:3:6; I:14:17;
I:30:68; I:60:11; II:49:84; II:50:50; II:64:104;
II:76:3; II:76:3; 0; I:60:11

Good luck.

3301

Steve remembered having heard this poem once. He searched for a few minutes, using various parts of the poem. By accident, he ran across a similar verse that pointed to the book *Liber AL vel Legis* by Aleister Crowley, also known as *The Book of Law*.

He deduced that the rest of the message pointed to different lines in each chapter of the book. This gave him a web address to a Dropbox and from this he downloaded an image.

"This is getting interesting," again, speaking out loud to no one but himself.

When booting from the image, a series of numbers started to appear, one after another on his screen.

2 3 5 7 11 13 17 19...

"Ahhhh. Prime numbers," he said while watching his screen.

The prime numbers continued to appear in succession on

his screen until they ended in "3301." Then the screen went blank for a moment and flashed, "The key is all around you." Then the image of the cicada appeared again.

"What's with the damned cicada?" he wondered out loud and pondered this next clue. Steve remembered cicadas from his childhood in Chicago; they all called them "17-year locusts," since they appeared every 17 years. He giggled at a long-forgotten memory of being outside on his elementary school playground, when the girls would scream at the site of cicadas flying and covering nearly every inch of the ground. So ubiquitous were these bugs that walking home that day, he remembered, every step crunched as his sneakers ended the lives of a half dozen or so of them.

"Steve?" His mother's voice from down the hall broke his thinking.

He looked up from the screen and yelled out, "I'm here in Dad's office."

A couple of seconds later, she said a little louder, "When you get a chance, could you make a trip to the station and top off the boat? I want to make sure we have enough before they run out during the holiday."

"Sure, Mom, I need to take a break anyway."

He snapped a picture of the screen with his smartphone and emailed himself the data he collected. Then he stood up from the plush leather chair, leaving the computer and all five screens on. Steve loved using his dad's office because Dad always had the fastest and most top-of-the-line computer. Dad also had an X-Box, another shared passion of theirs. He could have used his own laptop, but he was accustomed to using multiple screens, and Dad let him keep many of his programs on this computer for those times when he visited. *Mmm, obviously there was a method to his madness.*

This visit, he would enjoy a whole week of friends, family, and events at Clear Lake. It was a great break from his company. Mostly, he was hoping to connect with Darla King, who he heard from Darla's grandpa might be visiting. It would be a nice diversion, and who knew--maybe the sparks would fly again.

He closed his dad's office door and headed to the kitchen for the boat keys to complete his one task of gassing up the boat at the pumps across the lake. His mind wandered to images of a girl he had always loved, and of the cicada.

3.
International Space Station
21:30 G.M.T.

Lt. Colonel Randal Thomas Cunningham examined for the third time tonight the Automatic Telemetry and Guidance System, or ATAGS, on the International Space Station's US Orbital Segment. He had been in space six times on the space shuttle, before the sequester budget cuts scuttled that program. So, when the International Space Agency chose him over so many other fine astronauts from NASA, he was understandably excited. Other than the occasional practice in a jet trainer to keep some of their flight skills on edge, there was very little space travel to do as NASA astronauts. Simulations were fine, but they weren't space travel. The only opportunity for space flight was the ISS, if you were chosen, or with the Russians, who were not looking for skills as much as large cash payments for the use of their Soyuz-era rockets.

The telemetry was wrong again, but it didn't make sense. When his computers compared their data to that from Marshall Space Flight Operating Center in Huntsville, the readings were different. There had to be something wrong with either his computers or the orbiting satellites. He would have to reset ISS's computers, essentially a reboot.

"Damn," he exclaimed under his breath, realizing he was going to spend more hours than he wanted coordinating with Mission Control Center in Houston to reestablish a baseline. This work was the kind that R.T. found tedious, even if it was necessary. Still, it was better than being on Earth.

He looked at his mission clock, amazed at how quickly the time on this mission flew. It was his tenth "evening" in space. He just wished this mission didn't have all of these insipid technical problems, especially during the last few days. In less than five Earth days he would be heading home, and then, who knew when he would get another opportunity to go into space. Maybe never.

He wanted to take in every moment of his normal work, and not deal with computers. He didn't like dealing with his computer at home, and he certainly didn't want to mess with one in space. Naturally, this was the one big drawback of the ISS. Each of the crew did multiple jobs. With NASA, everything was about backup and backing up the backup. At any moment, there were fifteen ground-based technicians tasked with dealing with the shuttle's computers. Instead, he, a commander of three shuttle missions and now the commander here on the ISS, was doing menial computer testing.

Hearing a soft exhale of frustration, he looked to the left through to the next pod and saw Melanie, deep in her work. His whole demeanor changed.

Dr. Melanie Sinclaire was an astro-microbiologist with PhD's in astrophysics and microbiology. She was on board to study the effects of solar radiation on human tissue. Hers was chosen over many potential scientific studies submitted to the International Space Agency. Besides being a knock out, she made her field of study interesting. Plus, she also liked working late nights, analyzing her data and setting up the next group of experiments before they were to experience the sixth sunrise of the day. When in orbit, they averaged one every hour and a half. Mostly, he enjoyed working with Dr. Sinclaire.

"Evening R.T.," Melanie called out down the corridor

between her pod and the main one.

"Evening, Doc. How bad was the sunburn on Romeo and Juliet?" She named her rat pairs after famous couples, although he couldn't remember if the two she was looking at were Bogie and Bacall.

"Ha. That's good. I'm actually not as concerned about Samson and Delilah as I am about the radiation readings." Melanie rotated 180 degrees in her swivel chair attached to the side of the laboratory module so that she was staring at her computer screen. "Have you seen any of the recent ones?"

"Hang on, all my computers are being reset, so I'll come to you," R.T. said. He pulled himself up and over, sending his fit, 185-pound, gravity-free frame toward the port exit of the USOS, connecting to Melanie's laboratory pod. Then he poked his head through the entrance.

"Permission to come aboard?" said R.T., playfully chiding the formality of several of his fellow astronauts, who seriously asked this question each time before entering another's module.

"Here, look," she said, pointing to her computer screen, ignoring the levity.

He pulled himself beside her, enjoying their closeness. He only wished he could take in her fragrance, too. There was no sense of smell in space. Physics denied it.

"See? The readings are way out of the norms. You'd have to be three times as close to the sun to get these kinds of readings. I'm actually a little concerned about us. Have your computers given us any radiation warnings at all?" she asked, looking up at him.

"No. In fact, I'm having problems with my computers. I doubt this is a coincidence. I guess it's time to wake up MCC. You mind lending a hand?"

"No problem. Always happy to help my commander." Melanie added her own playfulness to cut through their pending computer tedium. "Besides, I want to get to the bottom--"

"Whoa, look at that!" He cut her off.

Melanie looked up and over to where he was pointing, to her left and out the aft porthole. They were both witnessing the most beautiful multi-colored aurora either of them had ever seen.

A sinewy river of green, red, and blue undulated and danced on top the Earth's atmosphere below them. The green part of the river expanded and grew past its invisible banks, like a time-lapse video of a flood, appearing to wash over the whole atmosphere. Most of it appeared over China.

"Wait, that's not the aurora australis, is it? Hold on. What are we looking at? Isn't that China? How is this possible?" Melanie asked. Her face was contorted in an exaggerated expression of both awe and concern. "That's nowhere near the poles."

"I believe we have a bigger problem than you thought." R.T. expressed what was on both of their minds.

4.

Dr. Carrington Reid
10:00 P.M.
Salt Lake City, Utah

Dr. Carrington Reid was predestined for this work, or at least it seemed that way. Like him, both his father and grandfather were solar astrophysicists and followers of Dr. Richard Carrington, an amateur astronomer who recorded the flare event on September 2, 1859, that bore his name. Reid's father was such a devotee that he named his son Carrington. His father would take him all over the world to exotic locations and observatories to study solar flares, pulses, and CMEs. Carr, as his father often called him, loved the excitement of the travel, but most of all, he loved the science. Science today was as the New World had been to Christopher Columbus; full of all the thrill and adventure of making new discoveries.

His interest in science and the thrill of new discoveries was indeed part of his genetic makeup, but his passion and drive were born from a desire to prepare humanity for a much anticipated cataclysmic event. Reluctantly, he was the biggest cheerleader and promoter of his own discoveries and theories, many of which were not shared by his peers due to their eschatological bent. His actions earned him a bit of a reputation, most of which was not good. He didn't care, as long as he achieved his goals of preparing the world and providing ample warning of the next Carrington-sized CME. This was why he had formed the CME Research Institute.

His thinking was that if he brought in other scientists and students, who shared a common focus of study--the deleterious effects of coronal mass ejections and solar flares on Earth's inhabitants--they would be able to learn more about the science and continually warn the world so it could prepare for the inevitable. Science was the necessary part of CMERI's mission; that included creating new advances in notifications when new solar flare or CME events occurred, as well as simply making new discoveries.

Dr. Reid's first notable discovery was on April 9, 2008, when he recorded an amazing cartwheel CME. He remembered it as if it were yesterday. A billion-ton cloud of gas launched itself off the surface of the sun and then did a cartwheel. It pirouetted out of the sun's limb in full view of the Kitt Peak National Observatory in Arizona, first doing a cartwheel and then a backflip: a gymnastic routine, which had never been witnessed before in recorded history.

He was the first scientist to show that the magnetic flux tube expelled from the sun began to heal itself, a magnetic reconnection also a first in recorded science. The data recorded from their Solar Dynamics Observatory (SDO) and from several satellites, along with staff comprising twelve scientists and students from the local university, formed the basis for his institute in Salt Lake City and the many discoveries he had made since.

Each event or discovery created an opportunity to share publicly, with warnings attached through his website, social media, and press relations. The press loved him because of his apocalyptic predictions and his "out there" theories.

Dr. Reid was also the first scientist to hypothesize that the Earth would experience a Carrington-sized CME within the next ten years. Many of his peers pilloried his theories and attempted to ruin his reputation, calling him a crackpot and fear monger. Although most had been silenced over the past couple of years, as many of his theories proved correct, few had embraced his dire prognostications.

Then in 2012 it happened. A solar flare bigger than the Carrington Flare by almost 50% was released. It was just dumb luck that the enormous CME emitted subsequently missed the Earth entirely. Had it been discharged a couple days sooner or later, the Earth would have been brought back to a new Stone Age. *We were lucky then, but it looks like our luck may have run out*, he lamented.

Reid looked at the data from multitudes of sources and the analyses from his scientists again and again, but the result was always the same. This time was one that he wished science supported one of his doubting peers and could prove him wrong. The current solar activity appeared to be far more excessive than had been estimated in this expiring solar cycle. He was frankly more than a little worried about the potential CMEs that were going to be launched. They might be even worse than the Carrington Flare—and that would be devastating to his generation's world.

5.
Miguel
6:00 P.M.
Rocky Point, Mexico

I make mucho people angry at me, Miguel Fernandez thought to himself, becoming more nervous about being late. This was the second time in a month he had caused his band to be tardy for a gig. Miguel was pretty sure Lupita would yell and dock their pay for it. His wife, Maria, would be disappointed and so would his band. Worst of all, Señor Max would be, too.

Miguel knew he was pushing it by spending that extra time with Maria and their unborn baby, Anna, who would enter this world in the next two weeks. He just couldn't interrupt his solo. It was his special engagement, at a far more important venue than any his band played, certainly more than Lupita's bar/restaurant. He was playing "La Consecuencia" to his daughter, whose applause was her happily kicking in Maria's abdomen. Then there were his wife's tender kisses of appreciation. There could be no better payment for his music.

Then, mindlessly, Miguel left his guitar by Maria's bedside and was a mile away before realizing it, causing Pedro to turn the car around to retrieve it. Pedro and Juan, his older brothers and part of Los Hermanos Mariachi, picked him up every night for work.

"Lupita is going to kill us for being late," Juan said, as Miguel got back into the car, this time with his well-worn guitar.

"Con permiso?" Miguel asked plaintively to his brothers.

Although Miguel was related to Lupita, that meant nothing when it came to the business of her restaurant. Lupita's closeness to Señor Max was the difference between Miguel's losing some pay and being fired. Miguel could not shoulder the loss of this job. With Maria not working recently because of the pregnancy, they were saving every peso they could get their hands on.

Praise Jesus for Señor Max. Max had always taken care of Miguel and Maria, starting with that first day they met many years ago, when he was barely 20, without a job, before Maria.

There had been a gang from the local cartel. For no reason other than Miguel's being at the wrong place at the wrong time, they started picking on him. Miguel had never run away from a fight, but this was four to one, and they had knives. He instantly grasped the trouble he was in and desperately looked for a way out, but there was none. The rest happened so quickly, it was mostly a blur. He remembered seeing one of the gang advancing on him with what looked like a machete. Then, this stranger he later learned was Max came out of nowhere. In less time than it took to recognize what happened, Max had removed their knives and reduced these "bad asses," as Max referred to them, to whimpering children who had run in fear for their lives.

He later heard a story that Max had made a personal visit to the cartel leader, returning the knives and making a payment of restitution. The cartel leader was so impressed by Max's *cojones* that he let him live, even though Max had embarrassed his people-- one of whom was the leader's son.

After this, Max had found Miguel and his brothers this gig at Lupita's restaurant, along with many odd jobs over the last few years. Recently, he and Max had taken trips to Max's ranch in Chihuahua or worked on his house at Dorado Beach. He never asked any questions, sure that Max was involved in something not quite agreeable with Mexican law, but otherwise, he knew Max was a good man.

Maria was another direct benefactor of Max's unending kindness by way of helping her to launch her cleaning business, before she and Miguel were even married. Max provided the materials to help him remodel their house, even helping him build what he called a "special room," that they still did not understand. No matter, they were truly blessed to have Señor Max looking out for them.

They pulled into the dirt parking lot and drove right to the back door, parking a meter away. Lupita was standing outside, waiting for them. Her angry eyes pierced holes through their dusty windshield, staring straight at Miguel.

They exited the car, grabbing their equipment sheepishly, and wasted no time heading directly toward Lupita.

"You're late!" Lupita yelled at her second cousin.

6.
Arrival
6:30 P.M.
Tucson, Arizona

Sally first saw her mom and dad on the remote monitor, walking down the concourse toward the waiting area. *First ones off the plane*, she chortled to herself while shaking her head in mock disbelief. *That's definitely Mom. She is the Type A of the couple.* "Everyone needs a Type A," her dad would always say in support of his wife whenever someone made a quip about their punctuality or one of her many lists. She was always organized enough for the both of them. Sally remembered when her mom readied her for school. Everything had a label: her food, her books, even her dang clothes. It was embarrassing.

As an adult now, she realized how great Mom's methods were. In fact, she had adopted many of the same habits throughout most of her professional and personal life. Perhaps that was why she was still single.

She thought her last boyfriend might be "the one," but after a fiery argument and breakup a few weeks ago, she was left to consider once again what she might have done wrong. It always made her mad after a breakup, with each beau essentially wanting her to change her ways to conform to his lack of willingness to change his own. What angered her most was that she was made to feel guilty. *Why am I the one who has to change? Was your life so damned perfect?*

She was starting to get mad again. This is why she thought a break from work and hanging at the family's Mexico beach house was a great idea. She was against it at first, what with Dylan's needs and all the work she had to do. During one of her weekly phone calls with Mom, she relented to the pressure of spending time with her family. Now, the idea felt great and the timing even better with Dylan out of her life.

All week, she had been excited about getting to the beach and spending time with both her mom and dad. Yes, she loved her parents and enjoyed spending time with them. The fact that Dar and Danny were coming later was the icing on the cake, or should she say honey on the sopapillas, since she was headed to Mexico?

There they were coming down the escalator together, holding hands, as always. The consummate couple, one of the many things she loved about them. She smiled, a wide smile, a Julia Roberts smile. *Could I really be this excited about seeing my parents? What am I, a freshman in college?* Her mom saw her first.

"There she is!" Lisa squealed "On time, just like I taught her. Honey, we are so glad you decided to join us," Lisa yelled as she dismounted the escalator, embracing Sally and blocking the way for all others to pass through the protective gate.

"Come on, you two, you're not the only people in the airport," Bill said, while inviting his daughter with his outstretched arms.

"Hi, Daddy," she said softly, accepting his bear hug.

"You wanna go to Mexico?" Lisa blared to her daughter and husband.

~~~

"You kept Stanley in great shape, honey," Bill shouted from the back seat.

"Thanks, Dad. I still remember the day you taught me how to tune up my first car," Sally hollered back.

"You having problems with the back window?" Bill strained forward against the seat belt, talking at the top of his voice to be heard.

"I'm waiting for a part from Mike. He says it should come in next week. Sorry it's so loud back there."

It was a lot louder than normal in the back of her 1992 Chevy Blazer. Its oversized tires, which were better suited to four-wheeling than highway driving, created a loud, vibrating ambient noise--especially at 75mph--that made it hard enough to hear, but additionally, the passenger window on the driver's side was open a crack so air screamed through the opening. He tried to close it but it was cranked as far as it could go. "Sorry, you'll have to live with that window being slightly open," Sally shouted after noticing Bill's vain attempt. "I hope you don't mind."

He didn't. In spite of its age and the occasional replacement of parts, like the window crank, he loved this vehicle. He had bought it new in 1991: bare bones with no extras. It was his first new vehicle, and he got it to go hunting with his buddies up in Wisconsin. He rebuilt the engine and even changed out the electronic ignition system for a more reliable points system. He liked a car engine he could work on in the field if a problem arose. It served him well for many years; ten years ago he gave it to Sally, who had inherited his love for working on vehicles. She babied it more than he had. Besides giving it the name Stanley (the reason for that escaped him), she tricked up the suspension and added the tires so that she could off-road around the deserts outside Tucson. She even kept their mechanic, Mike, who had to be about 70 by now. Bill had found him for her when he drove Stanley down to Tucson many years ago, so that she would always have someone to look over the vehicle when she didn't take the time to do so herself.

From the back seat, Bill could see all of Stanley's outward blemishes: window crank not working, seats starting to crack from years of exposure to the dry desert air, carpet showing its age and stains from the occasional dropped soda can of a passenger. Still, he knew the bones were in great shape. In other words, it was perfect. Sally made more than enough money to buy a brand new 4X4, but Stanley was a known commodity and it held sentimental value. She was proud of it and its connection to her father. He smiled at these thoughts and was surprised to see Sally smiling back at him in the rearview mirror, perhaps having the same ones.

"Are you sure Stanley is safe all the way to Mexico?" Lisa spoke up from the front passenger seat, barely audible, but intruding somewhat on their shared moment.

"Mommm," Sally exaggerated with all the drama she had when she was just a child. "You know how well I keep up with Stanley's care. Besides, I drove him down in January with Stephanie. Remember?" Sally's tone was defensive.

"Yes... ust ...ot ...re why you don't buy some--g ...this century that gets more than 10 miles to t—g--n," Lisa continued her new car argument, as she did every time she rode in Stanley. Bill was straining to hear the conversation, even though he'd heard this many times before. Lisa obviously didn't feel safe in an older vehicle; she didn't understand the emotional connection Bill and Sally had for this one. Besides, if there was a problem, they were much more likely to be able to get parts in Mexico for Stanley than for some of the newer vehicles.

"It's *sixteen miles to the gallon.* I thought you and Dad liked Stanley."

"We do," Bill interrupted. "You know your mom. She just worries about the 'what ifs,' especially when driving to Mexico."

Less than three hours after leaving the airport, Sally slowed down and pulled into the Indian casino parking lot in Why, Arizona, as always for a potty stop and so Bill and Sally could switch places. Sally didn't care for the Mexico leg, even though she'd done it probably 20 times over the years. Mostly, she didn't like driving at night after almost losing control, swerving to avoid a cow in the road some years back. It was long past sunset, and this moonless night was dark.

Less than a mile down the road, at the stop sign for the T intersection, Bill posed a rhetorical question, "You know what time it is?" He held out his hand. Sally, on cue, reached from the back seat and across her mom to the glove box and pulled out what she knew would be there--a much-worn CD case. Taking the disc from her, Bill inserted it into the player Sally added a few years back and put the Blazer into gear. He steered them south on Highway 85. The familiar beat started, with its guitars, steel drums, and then harmonica.

"Nibblin' on sponge cake. Watching the sun bake," all three sang out in happy unison, continuing the tradition they had started so many years ago. Always at this turn, when they were really headed toward Mexico, even though it was still 25 miles to the border and 89 to Rocky Point, they would start singing Jimmy Buffett's *Margaritaville*.

"Wastin' away again in Margaritaville. Searching for my lost shaker of salt. Salt. Salt. Salt."

Sally leaned back while mouthing the words that she knew by heart.

She opened her purse, anxious to take advantage of the last of her US cell service. She pulled out her iPhone and typed out a text message to her sister. "We're singing Mville now. Will b xing border soon. CU and D next week on beach. Pls email after this. Kisses."

She didn't realize it until later, but this was the last text message she would ever send her sister.

~~~

After passing through the military checkpoint around eleven, they headed east on Highway 37 about six miles to a turn-off down a hard-packed, sandy road for a couple of miles to a development called Playa Dorado--and their beach home.

Puerto Penasco, now known as Rocky Point or RP to the Americans who lived or vacationed there, had been a small fishing village a couple of dozen years ago. Because of its proximity to Tucson and Phoenix, land-locked desert dwellers flocked to Rocky Point for two reasons that made it unique and greatly desired: an ocean and beaches. The miles of sandy beaches and the Sea of Cortez's warm waters between Baja California and the western inlet of Mexico (and warmer still, the Mexican people) were a big draw for Americans. Infamously, Al Capone had favored RP for the same reasons. Those and its foreign port from which he could smuggle liquor through Arizona were appealing to him. Afterwards, mostly vagabonds, partiers, or anglers from Arizona or California were its frequent visitors until the 1990s when Mexican law changed, making it easier for foreign investment, especially in beach towns like RP. Then the building boom came, adding thousands of resort units and beach homes, drawing Americans from Arizona and California who wanted to buy into a paradise that was only a short drive away.

Bill and Lisa King had been coming to RP since their

college days at the University of Arizona in Tucson, only four hours away. When they were dating, they would come down with friends and party on Sandy Beach, now home to over one thousand condo units. Farther north was a new homeport for cruise ships, recently built by the Mexican government. Even when they moved to Chicago for Bill's job and later his current business, they still traveled to RP, even buying a home there that would one day become their place of retirement. Until then, they and Sally would enjoy it when each was able to, like now.

Like in most Julys, they figured that they would be among only the few "crazy Americans" who didn't care about the heat and wanted to celebrate July 4th on Dorado Beach. Sandy Beach was bloated this time of year with Mexican tourists who flocked from mid-country locations, taking advantage of bargain travel packages sponsored by the condo complexes whose units were offered for rental. Most Americans didn't care for the excessive heat during July and August, and often flocked to the cooler temperatures of the mountains or California beaches. However, most Mexicans, who had holidays this time of year, didn't care; they would rather bake on the beach than inland. Beach-home communities south of downtown RP rarely saw many visitors during the full heat of summer, especially the Kings' community of Playa Dorado.

Their beach house was modest by American standards. It was built of excellent materials and had many modern conveniences, but it lacked one thing that would seem so common and essential to most Americans. It was not connected to city electricity. Instead, it was outfitted with the latest solar cells, battery storage units, and a special A/C unit that ran so efficiently that if they were careful with their power, they could actually survive during the summer. With their pool, lots of shaded areas, and the warm ocean waters, they could enjoy their place even in the hottest months. For these reasons the Kings loved their piece of paradise.

Often, when Bill and Lisa came down, their next-door neighbor Max Thompson, as well as some of their other neighbors, would join in their many activities. Since the beach was always open, to afford themselves privacy Lisa's rule was simple: *When the curtains are closed, we want privacy. When they are open, come on over.* Besides being their neighbor, Max was one of Bill's and Lisa's best friends and certainly their favorite in Mexico. In fact, Max was like one of the family. This feeling carried over to their kids who all called him "Uncle Max." Max was the one who persuaded them to buy in Mexico after renting the house on the other side of him some 20 years ago.

Max also looked after their home, making sure everything worked properly and that workers did what they were supposed to. One summer, he even fought off a couple of drug dealers who tried to occupy the house. He never said how he did it, only that they would never be coming back again to bother the house. Bill knew Max had an in with the local police and maybe even the Federales, but he was always somewhat afraid to ask, honoring his friend's many secrets. With his connections, it was also not surprising that Max knew everything that was going on in Rocky Point.

Max was also a survivalist, but not the camo-wearing, ready-to-go-crazy-at-any-moment kind that most of the media envisioned. He was known as a "prepper," as in someone who prepped for the end of the world or for society's eventual collapse. Shortly after meeting Max, Bill came to understand he was buying supplies and storing up for the end of the world that he *knew* was right around the corner. Bill never knew where he kept everything, as his house didn't look that big. Nevertheless, almost every time they visited RP, Max had just returned from a trip where he bought

1000 MREs, or some sort of water storage tank, or 1000 batteries in hermetic enclosures. As far as Bill could tell, he was the only one Max shared this information with, including his end-of-the-world theories.

Right after they had built their beach house, at a party they hosted, Max shared over margaritas his concern about the coming zombie apocalypse. He heard of a new strain of the SARS virus and was sure it would manifest itself into something far worse than reported, turning everyone into brain-eating zombies. Then, a few years ago, it was electromagnetic pulse or EMP bursts from nuclear bombs, blowing up in the atmosphere and taking out all electronics, computers, power supplies, etc. Max was so sure of this, he even rebuilt his garage and a couple rooms of the house with something called Faraday cages around them. These would supposedly block out all the nasty effects of an EMP burst. Somehow, Max even persuaded Bill to do the same with one of his rooms when they built an addition, now their garage and office, onto their house two years ago. They both reasoned it would be the safe thing to do for their computer equipment, especially for Sally and her needs. At least that was the excuse he remembered using on Lisa to convince her of the need to do this.

Bill was not sure where Max made his money, but he was certain he had a lot of it. Not only was he buying top-of-the-line stuff, he owned the home on the double lot across the street, and Bill was pretty sure he owned more property elsewhere in Mexico and in the States. However, he couldn't remember Max actually having ever said this. Even more of a mystery was Max's past. Bill knew that he had been in the military at some point as a chaplain, and that he actually had seen some combat in Iraq. However, Max never bragged about his military exploits, so Bill never asked. The only time Max's tongue was ever loose enough to reveal some of the disconnected tidbits of info they had collected over the years was when Max drank a margarita or two with the Kings. Then, with one more piece added to a giant, colorful, thousand-piece puzzle, they would understand a little more about their friend. However, this was rare, and as far as Bill knew, Max never drank margaritas—or any other alcohol, for that matter--anywhere else. Defensive when asked, Max professed to love only Bill's margaritas made in one of those Margaritaville blender/ice shaver machines he had given to Bill as a 50th-birthday present.

Only once or twice, when Bill was sitting out on the patio or on the beach, did he observe Max drinking a beer, never more than one, but he never appeared inebriated nor did he reveal anything new about his past to Bill or Lisa then. Neither did Max reveal anything to anyone else he'd converse with. In fact, Max never really spoke to any of their friends about his past or anything personal. Whenever asked about something even remotely private, Max would adeptly pivot the conversation to something else. Once Bill asked about this, and Max simply said, "I'm embarrassed talking about myself."

It was because of their daughter Sally that Bill loved Max. Max always looked after Sally when she came down to the house, treating her as if she were his own daughter. He respected her privacy, and even when the curtains were open he never went over unannounced, except for one happy exception. Once, apparently, Sally had been in a very loud and heated argument with her former fiancé, Dylan, who thankfully she had since broken up with. From Sally's retelling, Max pretended that he didn't know she was there and that he came over to drop off cleaning supplies in their absence. Opening up the front door while knocking loudly, Max came in to find Sally's fiancé apparently about to strike her. Acting embarrassed, Max made a point of hugging Sally, and shook Dylan's hand so hard that he later claimed it was broken. She drove him back to Tucson that same day. Later, Sally thanked Max for his intervention and most recently for helping her to realize Dylan was a loser.

Also comforting, Bill knew that if any of the King family got into trouble in Mexico, whether it was with the law, or just paying a bill for the phone or water, which could be complicated sometimes, Max was always present to help. Whenever any of them heaped praise on their friend, he would say, "If you can't depend on your family, who can you depend on?"

From his last email, Max was making another run for supplies up north for a couple of days, so they weren't sure if they would see him until their big dinner in two days. However, Bill suspected he would, since Max had said he had something important he wanted to talk about. It was another Max mystery.

"Wow, it sure is dark tonight. Moon must be coming out later," Bill said, squinting to see their house coming up.

"22... 24... There it is, 26 Avenita Mar De Cortez," Sally said loudly. "We're home."

They pulled up to the dark front gate.

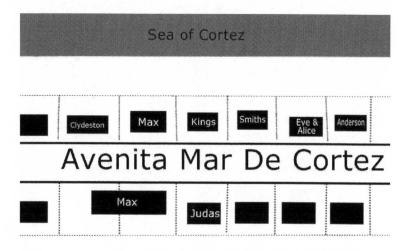

~~~

Meanwhile, on board the GEOS-12 Environmental Satellite in geostationary orbit 22,500 miles above Hawaii, the Solar X-Ray Imager, or SXI is routinely snapping one full disk image of the sun's atmosphere every minute. The results are sent automatically to dozens of research facilities and universities across the world, including CMERI's facility in Salt Lake City, Utah. CMERI's computers then process this along with other data from various satellites and ground-based telemetry, using an algorithm developed by Dr. Carrington Reid, to determine the severity of the 1 to 5 or more CMEs daily generated by the sun, and which are likely to hit the Earth.

To: Maxwell Thompson

From: bulletins@CMEResearchInstitute.org

Subject: 75% Chance of Carrington-Sized CME Expected

CME Research Institute
www.CMEResearchInstitute.org

BULLETIN
26 June

As we described in yesterday's bulletin, two large CMEs have caused above-normal aurora activity in both the northern and southern hemispheres. Auroras have been reported as far south as Wisconsin and Washington in the US, as well as multiple locations in China, India, and Russia.

A power substation in Anchorage, Alaska was severely damaged, causing power outages to most of the city still in effect at this bulletin's release.

Hundreds were killed in China from fires believed to be caused by the larger CME's charged particles, which caused geomagnetic induced currents believed to have reached more than 450 amperes to travel through local transmission lines, causing transformers to explode, touching off the fires.

NASA confirms that communications have been lost with the International Space Station and has attributed the loss to permanent damage to as many as three communication satellites caused by the dual CMEs.

We are tracking a third CME with less intensity, which is expected to hit Earth in 18 to 30 hours from now. There is less radiation expected, but auroras should be visible through most of the United States and as far south as northern Mexico.

Far more worrisome: one or more CMEs of greater intensity than last night's dual CMEs are expected in the coming days, as we have observed over a 5000% increase in sunspot and solar flare activities in the last three hours. Radiation readings recorded by the Hubble and the ISS prior to its loss of communications were the highest since such record-keeping was initiated.

From the most recent images received from the SXI telescope and other sources, we predict up to a 75% chance of a Carrington-sized event or worse to hit the Earth within the next few days.

We recommend that you take precautions immediately as outlined in our free downloadable eBook, _The Solar Apocalypse Survival Guide_.

Stay tuned for additional bulletins.

For more information go to www.CMEResearchInstitute.org & click on "Bulletins."

7.

Secrets Revealed
June 26th
Rocky Point, Mexico

The dark of night gave way to a hint of the coming day. A faint orange glow knelt on the edge of the horizon, separating the water from the heavens. Soon, the sun would stand up, revealing itself fully, setting fire to the whole sky and this part of the Earth below. Before noon, the temperature would already be near triple digits. For now, it was a perfect 80 degrees.

It was the start of a new day, a play that God puts on every dawn. His narrative by the sea is among the most mesmerizing. The audience stirs to the sounds of His actors: the birds calling out for food, the waves washing in from the Sea of Cortez, carrying with them a light breeze and pungent briny aromas, both alive and decaying at once. The sun, the protagonist of the show, rises slowly, taking its obeisant bow to its Creator whose hand slowly turns up the dimmer controls of the stage lights. In every moment, the backlight of this living stage changes. At any instant in time the change is imperceptible, but after a brief period, the day becomes brighter and brighter. It is a grand orchestra, playing a piece far more magnificent than anything Mozart could have written. Moreover, it happens every day in front of *their* beach home.

Bill could never describe how much he relished this

display. Nothing could match the feelings that stirred within when he witnessed God's amazing show each morning on the beach. It was why Bill always arose before anyone else to sit in his favorite chair, poised above and behind their sea wall between pool and sand, pointed south toward the beach. He sat in quiet awe, coffee in hand, taking in the bounty before him, wearing a never-ending smile.

He longed for the time when this would be his every morning. When he could sell his business and his only decision most days would be deciding whether to turn right or left on their daily beach walk. *Perhaps in a couple more years.*

A paddle boarder glided by, breaking Bill's mental meanderings, his sinewy form barely visible because of the great distance created by the low tide and Bill's tired eyes. The paddler waved and Bill waved back, not recognizing the man and not knowing if he had ever met him in person. That was the way of the beach. Everyone shared a friendly love for this magical place, welcoming to all others who shared their conjoint passion.

"Good morning, friend." Max's raspy voice came from behind, startling him like an unexpected ocean wave. He turned to see a beaming Max standing on the walkway their properties shared with a common waist-high gate. Lisa called it their "coffee gate." His bearded face set with a wide grin spoke of genuine happiness, but his eyes were full of worry, and deeper set wrinkles spoke of a lifetime of past concerns. Max stood on his side of the gate, holding it open with one hand and cradling a coffee mug of his own in the other. His mug, a gift from Lisa and Bill last Christmas, had "My other drink is a Margarita" hand-painted on it.

"Come on over. I want to show you something," Max beckoned his best friend.

There were few reasons that could drag Bill away from watching the sunrise. Max wanting to show him something was one. Max prided himself on his toys and maybe more so on offering anecdotes of how he smuggled them down through Mexico without getting caught or being forced to pay a tariff. He still called it *mordida*, even though the tariff payments were above board and not bribes benefiting the government officials extracting the tariff.

"Heard you pull in late last night in Stanley." Max took a sip of coffee. "I do want to say a quick hi to Lisa and Sally, but I've been dying to show you something and talk to you for a few minutes first."

"Sure," Bill said, now facing his friend, "they're looking forward to seeing you too. Maybe you'd like to join us for breakfast. Lisa is making chorizo and eggs."

"Damn, I would love to, but I've got some business inland with Miguel. Rain check?"

Bill nodded. "Of course, but you get to explain this to the ladies." He followed through Max's open patio door. Max spun around and curiously closed the blinds behind them and then both walked through the living room, coming to a stop facing a handcrafted, locally made wood bookcase, positioned at an angle between the dining room and kitchen areas. It was the showpiece of Max's home. Bill figured Max must have paid a fortune just to get it into the house. So large and heavy, it had taken a crane to lift it over the house from the street and a large group of workers to get it through the patio and into position.

"I've always loved this bookcase. Did, you get a new art piece or book?" Bill asked, glancing over each of the shelves for something new he didn't recognize.

Max said nothing, reached behind a book on the top shelf with his right hand, and pulled something that made a clicking sound. Then he knelt down, reaching into the bottom shelf with his left hand and pulled on something else that made a clicking sound. The whole bookcase appeared to shift slightly.

"No one knows about this, not even the workers who built this house. The few that knew of or considered its existence thought that this area is one of those safe rooms that *gringos* hide in when the crap hits the fan. But, you'll see why the secrecy in just a moment."

With this, Max pulled out on the right corner bookshelf molding, and all six hundred pounds of bookshelf and its contents swung open like a door to reveal another normal-looking door behind it.

From around his neck, Max withdrew a 3-inch metal rod with delicate silver teeth-like objects at its end and slid it into a hole in the door, just below the door handle. He turned it clockwise until a smooth but solid-sounding lock disengaged. He turned toward Bill. "This door looks mostly normal but it weighs 500 pounds, because like the walls it's reinforced steel, making it impenetrable to everything but a tank and C4, neither of which we're likely to ever see in Rocky Point. However, procuring and installing the locking mechanism was nearly impossible in Mexico. These latches are masterpieces of craftsmanship. Made of titanium, they slide up into the frame, also steel, and down three feet into the floor. Unless you have the key, there is no way to get in."

Max pushed the door in and they both stepped through. A neon light flickered for less than five seconds and then flooded the hallway with light. The hall ended in what looked like a large, unlit room.

"Now once you're in"--Max paused to make sure Bill was paying attention--"to make sure no one sees the doorway, you simply grab this latch on the back of the bookcase and pull in until the latches engage on the outside. Then just push this button here to unlatch the bookcase from the inside and push it open. You're not saying much, my friend. Are you in shock?"

"Uh, yes, I think I am. This really is amazing, Max. I can't believe how you did this without anyone else knowing." Bill was doing his best to take it all in. He had been throughout Max's house hundreds of times, and he never would have suspected the secret passageway and the long hallway before him, although his interest was mostly in the unlit room beyond.

"It did take a lot of *mordida*, but mostly it was because I used different workers from different trades, each of whom had a different job, so that no one really knew this existed. It took loads of money, planning and patience too," Max said as he walked past Bill and headed down the hallway to the dark room. Motion sensors caused the lights in the room to flicker and go on in similar fashion to the lights in the hallway.

"I cannot wait to show you my new toy. It was damn hard to get down here. I had to bribe one of the top dogs of both the *Federales* and the Ochoa drug cartel to have them close their eyes."

The room they walked into was very large, about the size of a two-car garage. It was two stories high and didn't appear to have any outside windows. Three of the four walls were covered in floor to ceiling shelving and wall-mounted storage. Along the fourth wall were a slick-looking desk and a comfy office chair on rollers facing several flat-screen monitors and other devices, the purposes of which Bill could not possibly guess. The whole area looked very high-tech, something that Sally would love to see. In the middle of the room was a large workbench, mostly clean except for something that looked like a cannon on top of it.

Bill no longer felt like he was walking on his own power. It was as if he were watching this from somewhere else. He could hardly believe that his friend had built this in Mexico and stored all of this under everyone's collective noses, including his own. Now Max was sharing this with him.

Max didn't wait until Bill turned his way. "Here it is." He stood behind the center workbench, on which rested the largest gun Bill had ever seen.

"It's a Barrett .50-caliber sniper rifle. It can hit a target at 2600 meters." Max picked it up by a handle connected to the middle top of the rifle.

"Holy Christ! That's like a mile away." Bill had already forgotten the secret passage and room, which was obviously where Max kept a lot of supplies. Now, he was completely focused on the monster gun. "A little jackrabbit hunting?" he joked.

"Ha. Not unless you like your jackrabbits in little tiny clumps. This is for killing someone a long way away, before he or she becomes a threat to you. Before the Barrett, only death and taxes were sure things." Max grinned at his quip but then continued with purpose.

"It's box fed." He detached the magazine and pulled out a bullet Bill thought looked like a mini missile. "I keep these here with the rest of my ammo," Max explained, pointing to an enormous steel safe. "All my other weapons are there as well. This safe opens with the same key I used on the door.

"See, you just push the magazine into the rifle until it clicks, and pull the bolt back, and... *Velado*. This baby is ready to take out the bad-guy."

"Max, why are you showing me all of this and how you load your sniper rifle? Not to mention the location of all your other guns, which I suspected you might have, and ammo, and the fact that it works with the same strange-looking key?" Bill was both puzzled and very worried.

"You're my best friend, Bill. If the shit hits the fan, I want you and your family to be protected." Max had already left the Barrett on the bench and walked around it so that he was facing Bill. "No one knows about this room or what's in here, except you. Not even those I bribed know what's here." Max paused a moment and then looked into Bill's eyes.

"Bill, if something happens to me, I want to make sure that you have access to this place."

"Max, first, nothing is going to happen to you. Second, even if it did, none of this would help me without your magic k--" Bill stopped and looked down as Max had just thrust that same key in his hand.

"This is yours. There is a lanyard on it so that you can put it around your neck. I have my own. Do not lose this. Promise me, you will keep it with you at all times whenever you are in Mexico."

"Okaaaay." That's all Bill could say as he was still processing all that he had been told, trying to figure out what this meant.

"Promise me, Bill."

"Okay, Max... I...I promise."

"And do not tell anyone, not even Lisa, what is here. You can tell her that you have a key to my house, which of course works all the doors as well, but do not tell her about this room. No one must know, unless of course, you need what's here. I'll leave that decision to you.

"One more thing. In the event of my death, I have left the LLC that owns the house to transfer to you and Lisa. Of course, as you know, like with your home, a Mexican bank trust owns the house, but you would essentially own it. I would also leave you some additional assets to make sure you can keep the place up. It's a bit expensive to run. Here is a business card for my *notario* who has all the details."

"I'm really starting to freak out here. Why all this? Why are you telling me this now? Are you ill?" Bill's eyes were wide and full of concern. He still held the key as if ready to use it, with the lanyard dangling down.

"Is that all you can say, my friend, after I told you I'm giving you all of my toys? Fine, maybe Clydeston would like my house. It has a bitchin sound system. Isn't that how the young people say it?" Max pointed toward his neighbor to the east.

"Stop the bullshit, Max. What's going on? You know, I love you as a brother. Why are you doing this, really?" Bill stabbed the key at Max like an accusatory finger, poking him in the chest with it.

"Okay, maybe bullshit is the correct term. Maybe I believe my own bullshit now. I'm just worried that the shit *will* hit the fan, and maybe very soon. There are just so many things going wrong for America and for the world right now. Call me paranoid, and I'm probably wrong, but I also realize that you, Lisa, and your family are my family. If something ever does happen, you get your ass down here and into my house. You'll be as safe as you can be. Besides, I just needed to be able to tell you about this. I've held this secret for so long, I felt like I was going to burst. I have no family, other than an ex-wife who doesn't want anything to do with me. Again, you are my family. You are my best friend, my brother." Max paused again to make sure he was getting through to him. "Will you accept this from me, brother?" Max thrust his hand out.

Bill considered his answer and everything Max had just said to him. After a long time he answered, "Of course, brother." Bill was quite relieved that his friend wasn't dying, and that Max just wanted to entrust his secrets to him. The threat Max mentioned was already forgotten, minimized like so many of Max's past warnings of doom. Bill stepped past his outstretched hand and embraced him with a hug. "Just don't die on us anytime soon. We need you more than we need your treasure-trove of toys."

"Deal." Max hugged back and released Bill.

"By the way, you never said if you were coming over tomorrow night. We should have twelve, including you."

"What, and miss our neighborhood association president, Clyde Clydeston, bloviate on something useless? Of course I'm coming." Max smiled that snide smile he had when he was going to say something a little off-color. "Besides, I hear Clyde has a new girlfriend with big boobs and she speaks little English. I wouldn't miss it."

"I can always count on you for so many things, Max," Bill said while putting the lanyard and key over his head for safekeeping as Max requested. The key pressed on him, feeling oddly heavy, as did the troubling thought that his family's life might one day depend on it.

8.
Sally
5 A.M.

Sally was tapping away on her laptop. Every couple of seconds, it would *ding* indicating that one of her followers on Google+ had just posted a comment in reply to one of her previous posts. She had already posted five times before breakfast, curating stories from the 'net, and pointing to an article she had written last week about the newest Samsung smartphone, published last night on the largest computer blog. Although she arose long before sunrise, having inherited the same sleep habits as her father, she didn't *need* to do any work.

She had pre-written all her posts and scheduled them for release at the rate of three per day during her vacation. Some were complete with video, including unboxing various products that she was blessed to see before anyone else aside from a few other tech reviewers like her. She also had four more articles pre-written that were being published over the course of the next two weeks on four different blogs including the one for which she felt the most pride, the Wall Street Journal Tech Sector. She had already done a ton of work ahead of time, so she didn't need to do any more.

However, she couldn't help it. Part of her drive was the desire to be known as the best in her field. The other part was her guilt in making sure that her 2.5 million followers on Google+ received the kind of cutting edge info they had come to expect from her, and of course, there were the sponsors. This was something new, so she vowed to step up her game when she signed up several sponsors, including two big-name gadget suppliers. Mostly, she just loved stumbling onto that esoteric story or two, which no one else seemed to know about. She felt like this era's version of Woodward and Bernstein wrapped up in one, without "Deep Throat," combing through the next big story. So, each day in addition to her "work," even while on vacation, she vowed to post at least two fresh things.

Sally's journalistic sources ranged across two hundred or so eNewsletters, thousands of posts and emails from followers, and hundreds of RSS feeds from the biggest to the smallest news providers. Personally reviewing all her sources would take her hours each day. Instead, she relied on her assistant, Brian, to do that work for her. She would then usually spend about twenty minutes, three times per day, doing a quick overview of these sources again using a program she designed and reviewing Brian's notes of suggested posts that he messaged her on her intranet site. That was the beauty of where she was. Brian could do a lot of the heavy lifting for her, and he even wrote some of the posts for her.

Brian was a find, fresh out of college, a blogger and Google+ devotee in his own right, with 50,000 followers. He was one of Sally's early followers right when Google+ started. He became one of her lead sources for new info, finding stuff she would miss. When Brian was about to graduate, he let her know that he was available, even suggesting the position and salary he would take to work for her. Sally actually hired him away from Google, who wanted him as well. Financially, it was a stretch, but it had paid off in spades when she secured her first few sponsors. Now, she couldn't imagine doing what she did without Brian.

He was a research hound. If you gave him a few clues, he could solve any mystery. This was very helpful when she would do some of her unboxing videos on new products. He would find out the details of what had led that manufacturer to make the changes they discovered when they examined a new product. He also had a similar knack for finding the stories that Sally had done on her own, which earned her so many followers. Now he was doing it for her.

She already had reviewed Brian's notes from last night and this morning, thanking him for it. There was nothing too exciting to report. In fact, Brian was going to post a couple of things on her behalf that were worthy but didn't interest her too much. Today, she wanted to have a little fun and really peruse her sources. She rarely had time to play the game, which was much more fun to her than lying on the beach. She was looking for the bizarre, maybe even the crazy.

"Massive blackouts in China point to US - Chinese tryst," she read from the Conspirator's Daily eZine. The author postulated a cabal between the Chinese and US Governments to sell more oil or some strange theory, which made no sense. However, in between the nonsense were two interesting points: blackouts affecting 17 million people, with some power stations down for potentially weeks, and sightings of auroras in areas as far south as North Korea.

She remembered seeing some story earlier which she had paid no notice to before, but with this information, she was captivated by its potential. "Where was it?" she asked herself while scrolling through her feeds.

"Bingo," she yelled out loud, abruptly stopping and looking up sheepishly, hoping her words were not as loud as she knew they were. She realized it was later in the morning than she assumed, and remembered hearing her mom making noises in the kitchen not long ago. Her sense of smell confirmed this, taking in the glorious aromas seeping into her room from the kitchen.

Looking back at her screen, she read the headline: *One of the largest Coronal Mass Ejections in years causes disruptions in China*. Not many details, but she knew she had found the trail she was looking for. She searched now for all news stories mentioning auroras or strange lights. This yielded quite a few results from the last 24 hours: *Beautiful aurora light show over India and China* by an Indian newspaper; *Strange lights reported in North Korea* by an alien conspiracy newsletter; *Vladivostok Ravaged by Fire – Many Deaths Feared*. She opened this one and read about large fires consuming almost a third of the city of Vladivostok, Russia, causing power outages throughout the city. Only one reported death, but many more were expected. Then she saw what she was looking for: "Several locals, just outside of the city reported seeing *strange lights in the sky* just before fires started ravaging the city."

Sally scanned through a few more stories with more than enough to post, but she was drawn to the magnitude of these results. This was a big deal, but it hadn't really made the news in the States. She was about to type out her post when she came across one more story, from thirty hours ago, before the auroras and CMEs: *Noted Solar Astrophysicist Predicts Global Apocalypse?* Not expecting this kind of story from her query, she clicked on the link and ate up the article.

A scientist named Dr. Carrington Reid, who had founded a research center that only studies solar storms, flares, and coronal mass ejections or CMEs, was being interviewed about a recently published paper. He posited that the most current solar cycle would likely bring about one or more CMEs that would be equal or greater than the Carrington Event that occurred over 150 years ago. He also stated that if a similar Carrington Event was to occur today, it would cause worldwide destruction and lead to the deaths of hundreds of millions of people or more.

Sally pondered all of this, ignoring her growling belly, and typed out her post: "Beauty & the Beast - CME causes auroras & destruction in southern Asia/Russia." Pointing to two of the best stories and the Dr. Reid interview, she typed, "A freak of nature or a harbinger of bad things to come? What's your take?"

Now she only needed the photograph. She learned early on that the old motto "A picture is worth a thousand words" is even truer when posting on social media or a blog. She first uploaded a stunning picture of a blue, green, and red aurora photographed in Alaska, since there was none yet from this event. But, then she ran across an HD video of a similar one, also in Alaska. Google+ automatically pulled multiple frames from the video and turned it into an animated gif, more literally a moving picture. It was stunning.

Very pleased with her post, her hashtags and links, and now the picture, she reviewed it all, making sure there were no errors. She then clicked Share to send her post to her 2.5 million followers worldwide, whether on their smartphones or their computers, as well as the millions of the Google searching public.

"That should get the nutters out as well. Always a fun crowd," she said, smiling and feeling good about this find.

She sipped some of the remnants of her coffee and watched the comments flood in almost immediately, one after another. *Ding* followed by another and another; her computer rang like a penny slot machine in Vegas.

"Great find, SallyKing," said Felicia James from New York.

"Wow! You rock, SallyKing," said Brian Santana. That was her Brian, who was always monitoring her posts, even on his days off.

"It's got to be the Chinese. They want our oil," said Frank Gomez from Texas. His profile picture was of a mustached and goateed young man wearing a Stetson and a vapid smile.

"I've been saying all along, it will be a massive CME that will take down society," said Wilber Wright, one of her favorite conspiracy followers and one of her many sources, in some unknown place in Illinois.

Sally closed her laptop and considered whether to walk out to the kitchen, knowing breakfast would be ready any minute, or to go outside through her patio door and see if Uncle Max was around. She could smell the spicy fragrance of chorizo calling her and her now ravenous stomach. Instead, she chose the patio door. She was dying to see if Max was coming to breakfast and get his take on the CME story.

9.

Wilber
7:30 A.M.
Somewhere in Middle Illinois

All right, Preppers, Wilber started his shared post for the Apocalypse Preppers community page on Google+. *This one is hot, coming from one of my favorite sources... 75% chance of a solar flare that will end all technology on Earth. If you haven't started your preparations, it's already too late!!!* This was linked via a shared post on his blog where he described the details of the CME Research Bulletin he had received and read about an hour ago.

"Wilber"--his wife's voice floated through his open window--"I think Petunia's got a cold."

Nut house! After a long exhale, he pushed himself up from his computer. "Coming," he yelled to the window and headed toward the back of the house to deal with yet *another* pig that probably had colibacillosis--the fourth one, now. He dreaded the thought of having to isolate her from the healthy ones, give her antibiotics and fluids, and clean out the pen *once again*. Olivia was on sick-pig watch, as she called it, quick to announce if one had diarrhea, a sure sign of this illness.

He walked the hundred or so feet from the back of their home down to the pigpens to the sound of Jumbo Jet, his favorite pig, already broadcasting Wilber's imminent presence to the others. He stopped for a moment and took in the view. Although not as incredible as the one from the front of their home, overlooking the main valley and town, his favorite view was out the back. The little stream wrapped around their home, below the pens and the stalls, and the sheer rocky face led straight up to where their windmill stood as sentry over the whole valley. They owned the biggest property in Ottawa County, some 1290 acres left to him by his family, and the only place he had ever called home.

Since taking over the homestead ten years after both his parents died in a car accident, Wilber had made quite a few improvements. Oil income from three wells in the valley had been taking care of their family's expenses for a lifetime. From the beginning, the Wrights were off the grid, as those from his prepper community would say, not because of planning on his or his parent's part, but because of the great distance from the town and its services. A windmill and solar cells provided all of their power needs, water storage tanks were filled by filtered water from their stream, and they grew, harvested, pickled, and stored their own food. He was just thankful that his family could take care of itself, which was much more important now than ever.

JJ, as they often referred to him, squealed once more, louder this time, announcing his displeasure at Wilber's repose. Pulled toward the mountain of tasks ahead, Wilber trudged forward with a grimace.

He really didn't need this. There was too much to do. He had to check the fencing on the eastern edge of their property, install the new part in the control unit for the windmill, store the shipments of ammo he had received yesterday at their delivery box, and go into town to buy some more batteries on hold for him at Dingle's Hardware. Finally, he wanted to work on the follow-up book to his survivalist novel, the one he was pretty sure was never going to get finished. But it was a nice distraction from what was to come.

He could feel something bad was going to happen. He didn't buy into all the conspiracy theories spread by the prepper communities he often visited to give and receive tips on making do on your own. Often reading reported incidents, which surely would lead to some cataclysmic event, Wilber would research further to check on their validity. Sometimes he posted some of the better ones, just to stir the pot. However, a number of the conspiracies made sense and seemed believable.

Lately, he had been reading lots of chatter about solar flares and CMEs, and it just sounded a little too real. Especially the reports from scientists like Dr. Reid. He knew they wouldn't be directly affected by the loss of power, but he was worried for his family's security. The whole town knew of his family and made up stories about the *Wrights did this or that* or the *Wrights have too much money and should share it with others*. It wasn't just the town's greed that kept him up at night. It was the fact that their food would run out and they would want to take from his family at some point.

Walking up to the pen's gate, he was assaulted by the smell of sickness. "Petunia doesn't look too good, does she?" Olivia said, cradling their baby on her hip.

"Thanks, O." He looked around, searching. "Where'd Buck run off too?"

"He's out trying to get that damned fox that killed some of the chicks yesterday."

Another thing he'd forgotten was on his list. "Can you do

me a favor and run into town and pick up my batteries at Dingle's? Buck can help me work on the fence today to make sure it's secure, if he ever gets back."

"Sure. I wanted to stop in to see Emma and see how she is doing."

"Tell her we're praying for her." He pecked her on the lips, turned, grabbed the shovel propped up against the fence, and entered the pen, starting his long work day.

10.
Stocking Up
7:05 A.M.
Rocky Point, Mexico

Max took a big bite of his burrito. Fragile wisps of steam emptied out of the bitten end, slithering by his face, slowed slightly by the brim of his blue Cubs cap, before emptying through the open air of his Jeep into the soup of the city's aromas. It was a blended mixture ranging from foul to delightful. A flavorful volcano of fire erupted in his mouth, an agreeable fire he doused with a big swig of the remainders of this morning's freshly brewed coffee from his large to-go cup. Eyeing his dwindling burrito as a predator would its prey, he bit through the soft tortilla, taking in another mouthful. Truly, very few things beat the taste of Pablo's burritos in the morning. He tried focusing on this diversion from what lay ahead for him and his friends. Unfortunately, it was also a reminder of so many simple pleasures that would soon be gone.

Max was sitting in the driver's seat of his Willys Jeep, left elbow resting on the door, hand holding the foil-wrapped delicacy. His right hand firmly held his plastic anti-spill coffee cup, or as Bill called it, his "adult Sippy-Cup." He mentally held back the onslaught of sounds and smells surrounding him, focusing instead on every morsel of the masterpiece crafted by Pablo's burrito stand, a few steps away from where he was double-parked.

The typical bustle of locals came by car, truck, foot, or

bicycle. It never took longer than a couple of minutes to shout their orders in Spanish while handing Pablo's wife, Maria, 10 pesos and then collecting their two foil-wrapped burritos from Pablo, leaving the same way they had come. It was the best deal in town for the greatest burritos. For less than $1 US, you would get two of either an egg-and-cheese or potato-and-cheese burrito. The only extra was a small container of salsa, homemade and equally tasty of course. The choices hadn't changed since he could remember hearing about this place over 20 years ago; always available only at 7:00 a.m., 6 days a week; and always a steady stream of customers. He learned that Pablo and his wife pre-made them and rolled them the two blocks from home in their handmade cart. Every day since their first day, they sold out, never deviating from the successful formula that served their family so well.

Max took another bite and then looked up to watch the steady stream of customers. He started unwrapping his second burrito.

He counted the traffic and calculated that Pablo and Maria took in about 2500 pesos in 45 minutes, which meant they had to make at least 500 burritos each day. Burrito production took the whole Garcia family, Maria told him, including their four kids, starting the assembly line at 4 a.m. They needed to purchase the cheese, milk, potatoes, and spices, and the foil for wrapping, but the eggs came from an uncountable number of chickens in their back yard. The tortillas were made fresh every night by Maria and their eldest daughter, for use the next morning. The pushcart was also homemade, a combination of Pablo's craftsmanship as a carpenter by trade and his father's design. Pablo Sr. had come up with the ingenious scheme of hollowing the chamber surrounding the metal burrito storage area. On the sides and below were sliding steel drawers, each with little grates, which held hot coals from a fire they prepared the night before. When filled and slid into place, the drawers kept the burritos hot up until the time of purchase.

Max loved stories like this one, but it was a common tale down here. He thought the Mexican people had far more ingenuity than most Americans he knew, which made sense since most had to live on and make do with a tenth of what an American typically did. Most Americans would just buy what they wanted, whereas most Mexicans made do with the used castoffs from Americans who replaced everything with the latest and greatest. Yesterday's big screen TVs, cell phones, computers, and so many other appliances that were tossed out or sold to thrift shops in Tucson or Phoenix, and from local vacation homes, ended up in the homes of many of the Mexicans here in Rocky Point.

Their ingenuity and lack of dependence on technology, Max thought, might give some Mexicans an advantage over their American counterparts when trying to survive society's coming downfall.

Max watched a pickup truck pull up behind him, barely stopping before pulling back out into traffic, leaving a tall, lanky, dark-skinned Mexican man who had hopped out of the bed and was already walking past the Willys to the burrito stand. He barked his order and handed a 10-peso coin to Maria, his new burgundy baseball cap nodding in the affirmative. The man grabbed his burritos and walked toward the passenger side of the Jeep, where he opened the door and hopped in.

"Hola, Señor Max." A full mustache made his teeth look even whiter than they were.

The Willys started to pull into traffic. "Hola, Miguel, right on time. Thanks for coming on such short notice," Max responded, seemingly focused on traffic and not on his passenger, who was already tearing into his burrito like a shark might take to a sea bass.

A couple of minutes later, they were headed first southeast on Highway 37 to Santa Ana. Then, they would head north before heading back south again on the small long roads that led to his ranch in the mountains. It would take about eight hours to get there and again that much time to get back. Max figured about two hours to drop off the extra ATV that was taking up space in his RP garage and pack up the trailer. If the police, military, and occasional drug gang checkpoints did not stop them too many times, they should make it back tomorrow, long before Bill and Lisa's party.

Max floored the accelerator and watched the speedometer hover at 80kph. The wind bellowed at him from everywhere, with only the windshield and side door windows abating the onrush of air already heated by the morning sun.

"Maria is not too mad at me for taking you away for a couple of days, is she?" Max yelled at him in Spanish, trying to be heard over the air screaming around them.

"No, Señor Max. You never wrong in her head. She just worried bout our little girl." Miguel shouted back in English.

"When is the big date?" Max switched back to English because it was still easier and because Miguel wanted Max to always practice with him.

"She say maybe fife weeks now. She get big as house." Miguel held his hands about three feet apart to demonstrate, in case Max didn't understand the analogy.

Acknowledging the humor, Max smiled back. His face then sagged. "When we get back, you tell her to stay inside the special room we built until the baby is born, okay?"

Miguel's expression darkened. "What happening, Señor Max?"

"I just want to be cautious, but I am a little worried. I won't lie to you. Just promise me you will try to keep her there, especially during the day?"

"Okay, Señor Max. Gracias for always take care my family."

The Jeep and trailer and its two passengers headed down the highway, already baking in the mid-morning sun, along a path it had taken many times before.

11.
El Gordo
3:33 P.M.
Northern, Mexico

Luis "El Gordo" Hernandez Ochoa was the third biggest drug lord in Mexico. Rising to become the ruler of a two-billion-peso-per-year illegal enterprise had taught him many things: use the talent God gave you; initiative creates opportunity; reward loyalty; and perform immediate cruelty to create respect and fear. He was as ruthless as his reputation. Nothing scared him and he feared no one except God. Raised in a devout Catholic family, he had learned what it meant to fear God and to watch out for signs. Like most Catholic Mexicans, his *madre* taught him first about signs. "There are signs everywhere, Luis, you just have to watch for them." She had taught him every day she was alive. However, it wasn't until her death that he came to believe in signs.

Five years ago, a competing gang seeking reprisals for his killing the leader's whole family had blown up his *madre* along with much of his villa. On that morning, he had awoken from a bad dream, where he remembered feeling sadness and loss. When his sweet *madre* was later blown to pieces, he learned never to ignore a sign, especially one in a dream.

Just moments ago, while sleeping through a hangover from alcohol and coca, El Gordo had awoken from the worst dream of his life. His dead *madre* was standing in the middle of a road that he knew well. While he watched, she threw the red hair ribbons she wore all the time into the air. Each ribbon fluttered upward, ascending with the wind, waving back at him. Then, the first and second ribbons combined and became a larger ribbon. Then, the third joined into the collective and so on. The growing mass of undulating ribbons transformed further into a fiery form in the sky. Each subsequent ribbon rose and combined with the burning formation in the sky. Now, he could feel the heat, and he started to sweat profusely. He looked down and realized he was on fire. He could smell that his clothes, hair, and skin were ablaze. He didn't feel any pain, but watched, horrified, as his fingers started to melt. His skin liquefied and then started sliding off the boney protrusions of his digits onto the ground below him. He could see that he was shrinking, becoming a molten pile of flesh and liquid. It reminded him of that American movie he saw as a child, *The Wizard of Oz*, with the ugly green witch melting. But faster, his mass was sliding into an El Gordo soup. He screamed!

In a pool of sweat, his silk pajamas and silk sheets soaked through, Luis sat up with a start. The mop of his black-dyed hair stuck to his forehead and covered his right eye. He pushed it away and hurriedly took an account of his fingers, his body, and then his vast bedroom. The partially exposed naked forms of two young women lay beside him undisturbed. The smell of his sweat and urine was overpowering. He had wet himself.

This was a fear he had never felt. Worse, it was without reason. *Why am I afraid and of what?* He considered this as he tried to calm his breathing.

Then, it hit him like a slap from one of his jealous lovers. He knew what he had to do right this minute, no, this second.

He swung his soaked flabby frame out of bed, and pulled

off his clothes, leaving a trail from his bed, as he ran to the shower with a swiftness his hefty body hadn't seen in years. He had purpose. He didn't know why or what exactly it was--only that he had to do it and do it now. He slapped the intercom button as he passed into his bathroom, heading for the shower.

"*Si Jefe*," chimed in his Number 1.

"Get the truck ready with Chaco and Bingo. We're going to the checkpoint in five minutes," he shouted, already in the giant shower, its jets automatically engaging and shooting hundreds of raindrops from all directions, drowning out the response from the intercom.

Four minutes later, Luis, his hair still wet, raced in his black Tahoe to the road he had seen in his nightmare. The afternoon light sparkled off the truck's gold highlights on the bumpers, molding, and headlamps.

None of his men asked where they were going, but they had their AKs at the ready for whatever trouble they must be headed toward.

"Who is covering the gate?" he asked his driver.

"No one today," the driver answered somewhat sheepishly, his lips and the scar on his cheek moving rapidly. "Remember, *Jefe*, the local police have been cracking down on checkpoints. We were going to wait for a week or two after Mayor Renaldo could say that he has been cutting down on crime and *mordida* to get our men set up again." The driver continued with a little more confidence. "Besides the cameras, as you told me, we have men every 200 meters around the villa and down the road. So if anyone comes, we'll know it long before they get close."

"Okay, thanks, Chaco. I can always count on you," Luis said, looking up to the sky but not seeing any red.

It only took five minutes before they were at the intersection where for years they manned the checkpoint on the dirt highway, if one could call it a highway. Only one vehicle every hour or two ever used it. People around here either owned a ranch or villa or worked on one. The owners paid Luis a protection fee at the gate to keep their streets protected from other gangs or crooked police. In truth, El Gordo wanted to keep tabs on who was coming and going near his residence. No reason why he couldn't make a little money off of his investment in personnel.

In the distance a cloud of dust approached from Hwy 2, maybe three kilometers away.

Luis got out and looked down each straightaway of the highway, the fear from his dream coming back. He just didn't know what he was looking for. It wasn't his *madre*, because she was dead, but maybe it was something or someone that reminded him of her. He knew he had to be here at this place, but he didn't know why.

The approaching engine and dust cloud were less than a kilometer away. He looked through the binoculars to see an old but familiar Jeep trailing an ATV. It must be Señor Max coming again to his ranch.

He liked Señor Max. He always paid his fee, kept to himself, and sometimes could get Luis weapons and other goods that no one else could, including a giant gun that could hit someone farther away than he could see. However, it was strange to see Max again. His men told him that Max had been to his ranch over a dozen times in the last two months. Each time, he transported supplies to his other house on the beach. Luis didn't care what this man did. Certainly didn't care if he moved his belongings back and forth.

Then it hit him as the desert heat on a summer day often slapped his face when he opened his patio door, before a dip in the pool. His memory was now crystal clear. Señor Max had always bought red ribbons for his *madre*. He didn't know what this had to do with his dream, but he was sure it meant something. Luis thought of his *madre's* face the last time Señor Max had handed her a ribbon, years ago now.

Max slowed and then stopped a few feet from Luis.

"Hola, Señor Max," Luis warmly greeted a surprised Max with his sweaty mitt.

Max answered the handshake. "*Buenas dias,* Señor Luis. It is an honor to see you here." Max tried desperately to show respect, while being genuinely scared to see the leader of the area's biggest drug gang at this checkpoint, always manned by someone at least four men below the boss in the org chart. *What the hell was he doing here? Now?*

"Not to worry, my friend. I was waiting for someone and I saw you pull up. Are you coming to get more supplies?"

Max hated that this drug kingpin knew his business so well, but that was part of the game he played and he certainly didn't have to worry about burglars. The Ochoa clan would dispose of any busybodies that ventured on to his property. Nevertheless, he wondered what would keep the Ochoas from taking from him, not that their offerings of protection services provided him with anything resembling a choice. He paid, without negotiation, because anything less would be suicide.

"Si, we're picking up supplies for my house and a few others in Puerto Penasco," Max offered, "Do you need anything, Señor Luis?"

"Thank you, friend, no. Seems like you've had to get

70

supplies a lot and such a far drive for you and Miguel to travel. I will have two of my men help you so that you can rest longer for your return trip."

"Oh, Señor Luis, that is a most generous offer, but I couldn't impose on you or your men..." "I insist," Luis broke in. "What kind of friend and neighbor would I be if I didn't help?" With that, he turned and barked a command to his men standing outside the Tahoe parked on the side of the road. Two of them started toward Max's Jeep.

Seeing El Gordo's men coming, Max realized his options were evaporating by the second. If El Gordo's men came with them, they would see all his supplies, what they were, and where they were stored. Everything was kept in one underground bunker with hidden access. Only Miguel knew its location and contents. Revealing his secrets to this drug kingpin would be tantamount to handing him the keys to his ranch and saying, "Take it all, please." What the hell was he going to do?

Max reached underneath the steering column with his right hand, feeling for a specific wire. He whispered to Miguel, "Play along with me and what I'm about to say. "

Miguel's face turned from frown to smile, recognizing with relief that his friend had a plan.

"Hola, Señor Max," one of El Gordo's thugs said, as he and the other climbed into the back of the Jeep.

Max found what he wanted, while turning to the man who spoke to him. *"Gracias Chaco, por su asistencia."* He pulled on the wire, and the Jeep's engine died. He turned his head to the ignition, feigning confusion, and then he tried the ignition. *Brum-rum-rum-rum.* Again, *Brum-rum-rum-rum.* Once more, *Brum-rum-rum-rum.*

"*Mierda!*" Max yelled and banged on the steering wheel with both hands.

"Miguel, take the ATV to the house, and get my tool kit and the ignition assembly on my bench in the garage. Here is the key." Max handed him an old key that Miguel knew wouldn't work any of the doors except the work area of his garage, where he would find the useless items Max just requested.

"Si, Señor Max," Miguel responded, then spun out of his seat and walked back to the trailer.

"Sorry, Chaco. I thought my ignition system would hold out till I made it to the house. It will take about two hours for Miguel to bring me the supplies I need and then for me to fix the engine. Do you want to wait with me?" Max continued his act while Miguel was already dropping the ATV ramp on the trailer.

"*Jefe? Con permiso, Jefe.*" Chaco and the other man, who said nothing, were out of the Jeep and jogging to Luis, catching up to the portly cartel king while he was talking to his other thug.

Max got out, popped the hood, and acted as if he was starting to repair the ignition.

Chaco turned back and jogged up to Max and Miguel, who had pulled the ATV up to the front of the Jeep and was acting as if he was getting further directions.

"El *Jefe* say, he sorry, but we are needed on other duties right now, unless you need further help with your engine," Chaco said, out of breath.

"Tell Señor Luis again, thank you for your offer of help, but we'll be fine."

With that, Chaco turned and left, and two minutes later the Tahoe pulled away in a trail of dust leaving one of the three guards, the man who had accompanied Chaco but hadn't spoken, standing by the makeshift gate El Gordo and his band of thugs maintained at times.

Max turned back to Miguel and said quietly, "I'm sorry, Miguel, but you're going to have to go back and pull out the major supplies I told you about by yourself and put them in the garage. After an hour, get the things I mentioned and race back here. I'll pretend to work on the Jeep while you're gone. With luck, none of El Gordo's men will want to accompany us, but if they do, we'll show them only the garage and the house. Got it?"

Miguel nodded and accelerated the ATV like a crazy, drunk tourist on spring break until his image and the sound of the engine disappeared in the dust cloud down the road.

To: Maxwell Thompson

From: bulletins@CMEResearchInstitute.org

Subject: WARNING - 90% Chance of Carrington-Sized CME Expected

CME Research Institute
www.CMEResearchInstitute.org

BULLETIN

27 June

WARNING

We are sending you this warning because we are now 90% sure that a Carrington-sized event will occur in the next 36 to 60 hours.

At least one CME (and maybe more) is expected to reach Earth within that time.

We strongly recommend that you plan on many weeks or months without power or services. Stock up your food and water. If you are in the city and you can make it to a more rural area, we recommend you leave now. Do not wait. You no longer have time.

Stay indoors when the sun is highest in the sky, as you will be subject to anywhere from 500% to 2000% the normal radiation level that you would receive on a normal day.

All of these and other recommendations are listed in our free downloadable eBook, _The Solar Apocalypse Survival Guide_ .

We will continue to transmit bulletins as long as we are able.

For more information go to www.CMEResearchInstitute.org & click on "Bulletins."

12.
Onboard ISS
10:00 G.M.T.

The last time they received communications of any kind it was not good. Both NASA and the European Space Agency warned of severe disruptions or worse from the CMEs that were pounding Earth and the larger ones coming their way over the next few hours or days. Thankfully, although their communication equipment was useless, their other systems were functioning and fairly well protected against the coming onslaught. The other five astronauts were going about their normal duties, as well as double-checking the ISS's safety protocols and the two escape capsules to make sure that nothing was missed, in case they had to bug out quickly.

They were about as protected as they could be, with their shielding specifically designed to take massive doses of radiation while in orbit above the protection of the magnetosphere surrounding the Earth. Otherwise, they would have already left for terra firma.

Their larger concern was how Earth would fare in the next day or two. From what R.T. read from the last CMERI Bulletin, the one or more CMEs headed to Earth were among the largest ever recorded and they were coming fast. Assuming they were as large as estimated, the devastation would be enormous. He remembered reading a book called *EMP: The Escalating Threat of an American Catastrophe* that described what would happen if an

EMP from a nuclear bomb or CME were to hit North America. All power would be out for months, years, maybe even a decade. The world as they knew it would be over. All they could do now was wait and see what happened. Wait, and pray.

R.T. stared through the porthole before him at the seemingly benign colorful clouds below, and he felt utterly and completely helpless.

13.
More Prepping
4:30 A.M.
Rocky Point, Mexico

Upon returning from his ranch, Max unloaded Miguel and a few of their supplies at Miguel and Maria's home in town. Then he headed back to his own beach home. Max never noticed the late model Chevy truck that had been tailing them the whole way down. He had other concerns.

About four hours before reaching Rocky Point, Max had noticed a tweet on his phone. It must have downloaded when he had WiFi service at his ranch house, since he didn't subscribe to Internet data on his phone. The tweet was from @1859Storm, one of the Tweeters that he followed whose avocation for following CME data was better than any solar physicist's, except perhaps Dr. Reid at CMERI. This tweet was one of his many daily tweets reporting each day's number of CMEs. It read: *#CME summary: 15 coronal mass ejections in past 24 hours. (For updates visit: http://t.co/KlepA5unnr).*

"Wow, fifteen in one day," he had said out loud, but not loud enough to wake Miguel who was sleeping off the previous day's work in the front seat. The sun normally emits anywhere from one to four CMEs during solar maximums and one every other day during solar minimums. They were definitely in a solar maximum, so multiple CMEs were expected each day. However, this number was completely unprecedented.

Max couldn't open the picture because of his lack of Internet connection. He considered this and all the other bulletins, emails, and tweets he had received over the past couple of days as he turned onto Avenita Mar De Cortez.

He was no scientist, but he knew all the information was pointing to one thing. He was out of time. They all were.

He pulled into his other house across the street from his beach house, what he called--to himself--his *beach warehouse*. It sat on a double lot between other lots already graced with two- and three-story edifices, all outfitted with many windows and terraces designed to afford sweeping views of the ocean over the on-the-beach homes, like those owned by Max and the Kings. These weren't technically beach lots, because they were on the other side of the street and their views were obstructed by the beach houses in front, so all were half or a third of the price of similarly sized homes on the beach. This made beach living affordable granting many, with the lower cost labor and materials in Mexico, the ability to build big without the hefty price tag of a lot right on the beach.

Max's lot and structure were built for a wholly different purpose, but were designed to look similar to all the other homes on either side of him. His structure was three stories as well, but instead of a typical second-story master bedroom with furniture positioned to take advantage of the stunning sunrises and sunsets, the large room contained the top of a 2-story 100,000-gallon gravity-fed water supply tank. It sat on a reinforced concrete pad hefty enough to support a 15-story building. Built around this, the rest of the house comprised an enormous warehouse and a two-bay garage that were reinforced in case of attack, caged against an

EMP, and insulated to protect the contents from the extreme heat of the Sonoran Desert summers. In the warehouse, he stored enough foodstuffs and supplies to feed and outfit an army, or in this case, enough for two years of survival for him and his only family, the Kings.

The master bedroom, besides having two feet of a water tank protruding through most of what would be the floor, had a spiral staircase leading up from the ground floor and going up to the roof terrace. Inside, the only furniture in the few unused square feet was a lounge chair placed in front of the sliding glass window and balcony, which faced the beach and ocean. Sometimes, when the Kings weren't in their house, Max would park himself in this chair and enjoy the views and peace its isolation offered him by not being directly on the beach. Some nights, he found himself sleeping in what was probably his most comfortable chair. Then he would wake up with the window open to the sounds of the ocean and the lively aromas brought in by the breeze. He also felt safe here, even though it wasn't as protected as his safe room in his beach house, but he loved the ability to see miles in each direction, especially from the terrace above.

The terrace on the roof provided the best views of everywhere surrounding their homes. There were two chairs underneath a canopy for protection against the sun, from where he could see any approaching combatant. Others around him built their top-floor terraces to soak up the sun and the ocean, whereas Max had built his terrace specifically to afford the best vantage point if someone or some group attempted to take what he and the Kings had. Elevated above everyone else's terraces for protection and secrecy, Max's terrace had reinforced walls that could withstand bullets and an inside threshold on which the bipod of his new sniper rifle currently rested, with a special weather-proof cover, mostly protected from an unknown enemy below.

14.

Darla
6:40 A.M.
Clear Lake, Michigan

A light breeze blew. One by one, the sounds of morning announced the coming day: the flapping flags flying from their flagpole signaling homage to the US, the state of Michigan, and the Fighting Irish of Notre Dame; the calls of sparrows going through their morning rituals; the approaching roar of a jet ski slicing through the calmness of the lake; the water lapping against the seawall from the newly created waves. These sounds were part of the melodic music Darla King knew as summer at her grandparent's lake home.

Like her parents, when she was able, Darla loved spending the first part of the morning by the water. When visiting Mammie and Poppy, she did so on one of the wooden Adirondack chairs, with coffee in hand, taking in the view and smells of the lake.

At the last minute she had decided to make the quick journey to Clear Lake, figuring it would be good for her and Danny. He was off, plus she was done with her schooling until next semester and her aerobics class was finished for the summer as well. *Why not get the vacation started right away, visit the lake and then back to Chicago late tomorrow before flying to Tucson and then connecting through to Rocky Point to meet up with Mom, Dad and Sally.* She would make any excuse to visit the water.

She loved the water so much that when she graduated from

University of Illinois in Computer Science, she planned to get a job in California or Florida or any place she could be by water all the time and be warm. Like her mom, she hated the cold. Michigan was beautiful during the summer, but it sucked during the winter, and so did Chicago.

The sound of an older throaty engine echoed on the lake, then grew louder as the old girl announced its approach with pride. A classic Woody promenaded past, its occupants happily waving at Darla. She didn't recognize them.

The community surrounding Clear Lake was a close-knit one, so it was not surprising that every third or fourth jet skier or boat's occupants waved at Darla. Most remembered her, her sister and their brother from their parents' bringing them here over the years. Just like her parents, everyone seemed to know her grandparents. That meant lots of people would be coming by to visit, even during her short stay. Darla never minded. In fact, she thought it was pretty cool that so many people cared about her and her family.

Another engine sounded. This one was testosterone-filled, its pistons pumping more rapidly. Within a couple seconds, it shot into view. This time, the driver was someone she recognized. Steve Something. *Cute*, she thought to herself, as Steve Something drove by waving. She couldn't help herself. Grabbing her Droid, she surreptitiously snapped a photo of him and his boat while waving with her free hand. For just one moment, her eyes locked onto his, her heart fluttered, and then Steve passed out of sight. She opened her mail app and started typing out a message to Sally.

OMG, I just saw Steve-I-Can't-Remember-His-Name... You remember him, my knight in shining armor who saved me many summers ago. I also don't remember him being that cute. Of course, we've both grown up since then.

Darla added the picture to her email.

He just boated past me in a...

She squinted at the picture, trying to remember the model. A quick search with her phone gave her the answer: a Cigarette 39 Top Gun.

... Cigarette 39 Top Gun. Not sure which was hotter. Wish you were here. See you in a few days.

Love, D

She pressed the Send button and smiled at the *swoosh* sound.

"Can I join you?" Her grandpa was still wearing his pajamas but looking stylish in them.

"Sure. Good morning, Poppy." She pushed up from the chair, making a smoochie-face and accepting his kiss on her cheek.

"Was that Steve Parkington who passed by in the boat?" He asked, taking the chair next to Darla.

"Parkington. I forgot his last name. I don't remember him being that good looking. I hope we'll get to see him while I'm here."

"You will tonight," Fred King grinned at granting his granddaughter's wish. "Steve and his parents, John and Uta, will be here. They're all coming over for tonight's barbeque."

"Really? Awesome. I'm glad I brought a proper swimsuit with me. I remember Steve, of course, but I don't remember his parents," she declared, trying to redirect her Poppy's knowing looks off the subject and taking the last sip of her coffee.

"You might recall they were over two summers ago when you were here, although Steve was probably in school at UM then.

He's graduated now and runs his own company full time. John and Uta live here, but they work in Detroit. She's a manager at the large power plant there, and John owns some sort of computer company that has something to do with sharing pictures on the Internet, I think."

Oh yeah... Picshare. I love that app on my phone, she thought, really glad she made the trip.

"Your old friend Stacy Jenkins is coming over, too. You ought to talk to her about sharing a ride with you to O'Hare tomorrow night. I think she's flying out around the same time as you."

"I haven't seen Stacy in a while. I don't know if we will be able to share a ride, unless she can get one back, because Danny has to get to school when we get back after the holiday. But maybe we can at least caravan and share a beer at O'Hare. This trip is getting better and better."

"Oh and there's a surprise," he said with a smile, letting the suspense build until Dar was practically bouncing of the chair. "Tonight is Clear Lake's fireworks show."

"Wow! Awesome, I love fireworks!" she said gleefully, clapping her hands.

"I know." He couldn't wait to tell her this when he heard she was coming to visit them, knowing how much as a kid she loved *oohing* and *ahhing* at the fireworks displays on the Fourth.

"Speaking of fireworks," she furrowed her brow, "did you see the funny colored lights last night? I thought maybe it was fireworks, 'cause my bedroom was lit by all these colors and lights, but I didn't hear any sounds. I was half asleep and was trying to figure out what they were, when I fell back to sleep, thinking how beautiful they were."

"I'm sure it must have been the Woos next door. They always have great fireworks. They were probably shooting them off last night, but it's weird that I didn't hear them either."

15.
Prime Numbers
6:50 A.M.
Clear Lake, Michigan

"Prime numbers!" Steve Parkington yelled to the morning. This revelation hit him while thinking about yesterday when his little nephew had delighted in the act of squishing bugs in front of his sister, eliciting shrieks from of her with very little effort, just as Steve used to do when he was a kid during the plague of cicadas.

"Why didn't I think of it the first time?" he chided himself. *The key is all around you*, the message said. He reasoned that the cicada had two known life cycles, 13 or 17 years. Both were prime numbers. The prime numbers listed on the final screen going all the way to 3301 and the cicada's life cycle both pointed to some sequence of prime numbers.

Steve turned off the boat's engine, and in one fluid motion hopped onto his parent's dock while holding the mooring line. He pulled the boat to the dock and then tied it off, quickly and precisely. His mind and body buzzed with excitement from both figuring out the answer to the puzzle and seeing Darla King. She looked great, sitting in the lounge chair sipping her coffee. He couldn't wait to meet her again, tonight.

They had played as kids so long ago. He was secretly in love with her then, but she was so popular and beautiful, and he was still in his nerdy phase, with glasses and unkempt hair and clothes. Then, a couple of days ago, his father told him she might be at the barbeque. He looked her up on Facebook, surprised at how the years had turned her into such a beautiful woman. But he didn't friend her, although he couldn't at this moment remember why. He would cross those bridges tonight, but now it was the cicada and he had to share it with his father.

He stopped his jog at the patio door and then walked briskly to his father's study to talk to the man who shared not only his genes but also his interest in puzzles. Together, since finding the clues, they tried to figure out what it all meant and where it would lead.

Steve opened the office door and found his father sitting behind the same desk that he himself had sat at two days ago while trying to crack the cicada code. The largest of the five screens had a map with a virtual pin on it. His father was grabbing what appeared to be a color printout of the same map.

He turned to the door where his son was standing. "Hi, just the man I wanted to see. We solved it, Son."

Steve was eager to hear, but also disappointed at the same time, knowing his father just figured it out too.

"It's GPS coordinates somewhere near Boulder, Colorado," John said, handing the printout to his son. "It was the cicada that pointed to the prime numbers–"

"I know, the life cycles of 13 and 17 years. That's why I came in here, 'cause I just got it," Steve said, while looking up from the map.

"Yes." John picked up the thread. "I was looking at the prime numbers and the other cyphers you figured out. They pointed to specific GPS coordinates, which when entered gave us this location."

"But, what's there?" Steve asked the obvious.

"I have no idea. You want to go find out?"

"Duh. When do we leave?"

"I have a little business first," John paused, "but then we'll take the Cessna early tomorrow evening to Denver and then a rental car to these coordinates." He made an exclamation point with his finger, jabbing onto to the pin of the map he had printed. "What do you think? Sounds like a great adventure, doesn't it?"

"Dad, that's awesome. Great work," Steve said with less enthusiasm than John had hoped for.

"Everything okay? Thought you would be more excited." Then it occurred to him. "You're really looking forward to seeing Darla, aren't you?"

"Busted," Steve said, feigning embarrassment. "There is a reason why most of your friends call you the smartest man they know. When can we head over there?"

"Your mother had to go back to work because of some problem at the plant. Everyone else will be at the dock ready to go at one."

"Great," Steve beamed. He was filled not only with the joy from their mutual accomplishment and the upcoming sense of adventure, but with his eagerness to see Darla.

16.
Fireworks
1:20 P.M.

He saw her the moment they pulled alongside the Kings' dock.

She was radiant, far more beautiful than he ever remembered. She wore a red, white, and blue bikini, with a wrap around her waist. Her hair was long and black, and it shone in the afternoon sunlight. Her smile, punctuated by her pretty red lips, preceded a laugh that she bellowed at two girlfriends facing her. Her voice reached their boat, flying to him like the beautiful song of a rare bird. *Wow*, he thought, *she's gorgeous.*

They tied up alongside another boat already docked, but unable to wait any longer Steve dove into the cool lake water.

After his son's head broke the surface, John yelled, "Hang on, Steve, can you grab the cooler?"

"Sorry, I'm coming," the boy hollered back from the dock a few moments later.

As he pulled himself out of the water, he realized his suit clung to him somewhat more snugly than he would have wanted. Tugging on his suit edges, he looked up and saw Darla and her two friends, now quiet, staring right at him. A blush heated his cheeks. He smiled, quickly turned and walked over to their boat already tied to the dock. His heart racing and his face red, he reached for the large cooler his father handed him.

Darla was beside herself with excitement, ignoring the giddy schoolgirl remarks from her friends, watching him grab a cooler from his father and walk down the dock toward her. She had thought he was cute when she saw him in the boat this morning, but *he turned out to be a major hunk.*

She smoothed her wrap and simultaneously combed back the right side of her hair, pulling it over her right shoulder. "Do I have anything in my teeth?" she whispered quietly to her friends, who were now ignoring her and watching Steve approach. They all waited, breathless.

"Hi, Darla. I don't know if you remember me from years ago. I'm Steve," he said with a slightly shaky voice, making hesitant eye contact with her.

"Hi, Steve," she said. "How could I forget? You saved my dignity when we were kids and my top came off when we were diving off this very dock. Your friend Robbie Benson wouldn't give it back to me, even after I begged him. You threatened him. It was something about his braces..." she trailed off, trying to remember.

"Wasn't my friend. I told him I would pull his braces out of his mouth with pliers if he didn't return your suit. No wardrobe malfunctions today, I see." He hated himself for saying this, not wanting to sound like he was only interested in her body. He tried hard not to let his gaze drop from her eyes.

"No, and it looked like I wasn't the one having trouble with my suit today," she said smiling.

"Are you here through the Fourth?" he asked in a desperate attempt to change the subject.

"No--" she started to reply, but a voice behind her interrupted.

"Darrrrrr! Grandpa wants you to go to the store to get something."

"That's Danny, my brother. Ahh, we leave really late tomorrow night. We're flying to Mexico to meet my mom, dad, and my older sister in Rocky Point." She paused, distracted. "Sorry, but I have to go run an errand for my grandfather..." She smiled and her eyes twinkled. "You wanna come?"

Of course he agreed, after apologies to his dad, who was helping Dar's grandfather Fred with the BBQ duties. She drove and talked almost the whole way to the Clear Lake Market and back. She talked about her final year of studies, what she planned to do in the IT field--one more interest they shared--about where she wanted to live, and her family. They compared their travel plans for tomorrow evening and how their planes might even pass each other in the air, even though Steve and his dad were flying much earlier than she and Danny. He enjoyed her every word and felt the time breeze by just listening. She loved how he listened to her so intently and how he answered her questions with confidence. Before they knew it, the round trip was over in twenty minutes.

Later, after each had made rounds with their mutual friends, swum, and eaten with their respective families, long after the sun had set, Steve and Darla ended up in two Adirondack chairs next to each other. Their conversation picked up where it had left off, and they continued non-stop, pausing only to listen and sip on a cold beer. They were completely captivated by each other's words.

"What time do the firew...whoa, look at that. That looks like an aurora," Steve pointed at the northern sky, about where the fireworks should be discharging at any moment.

Two wispy, shimmering, green clouds slowly snaked along the horizon moving toward them and to the west.

"Yeah, you're right. I saw an aurora during an Alaskan cruise with my family many years ago, but it's kind of rare to see them here," she said, face pointed more toward him now.

At any other time, the auroras would have been ominous to both of them, but a larger force was at work.

The aurora's green light illuminated her face, lifting the veil of darkness which had covered them both for the past few minutes. She wore an expectant smile, which was even more alluring because of the green vaporous radiance above. He could not restrain his feelings for her any longer. Leaning closer, he kissed her.

First surprised, she was quickly fully accepting.

Slowly, he pulled away. "I'm sorry, but I've wanted to do that since I first saw you." He sounded repentant, but felt no regret.

She kissed him back.

When the Clear Lake fireworks started, both smiled at each other, not just from the pleasurable kissing they had shared but because they both felt like they were part of an overdone ending to a romantic movie. Wanting more, they kissed each other again.

The foreboding green auroras were lost in the smoke and haze of the fireworks, and any concerns about them were lost in the fog of their kissing and newfound love.

17.
Worrying
7:20 P.M.
Rocky Point, Mexico

As Max finished unloading his supplies in the warehouse, carefully stacking them in their allotted areas, he was lost in thought considering if he forgot anything. He felt like he had done just about everything he could to provide for their survival of what he knew was coming perhaps as early as today.

He just wished he could do something for all the others. So many would die from what was about to happen. Not right away, but months from now. Mexico would be a little better off than the US, but even this generation of Mexicans was more and more like their American counterparts, relying on supplies and services that were delivered just-in-time. This method of delivery was very efficient in a diverse, global economic world with lots of technology. However, it meant when the delivery systems stopped, people on average only had a week's worth of food and even less water.

When the panic started, not at first, but in a few weeks, fueled by a realization that help was *not* on the way and their fear and pangs of hunger began to take over, then it would get really ugly. Neighborly love and friendship would be replaced with a drive for survival, not only for self, but also for one's family. However, what really caused Max to lose sleep lately was the result of when weeks turned into months. That's when the mass deaths would occur. What lives weren't taken by disease, which would be rampant, would be lost when neighbors killed neighbors for a few morsels of food, or even one drink of water. Then there would be the gangs. Human nature included the ability to commit deplorable acts against one another. Those wired with one too many Y chromosomes or with a few extra brain cells and a Napoleonic complex would assemble like-minded miscreants, who together would rape, murder, and take from others.

He dreaded those days, which he knew were as inevitable as each day's sunrise and sunset. What would he and his friends become when they took lives to protect their own? Would they become the cold-blooded murderers he reviled? Would they eventually forget their humanity and their love for others, being only concerned for their survival at all costs?

He believed that these concerns separated him from the extreme survivalist, who desires the apocalypse, drawn by a longing for a license to murder with impunity and embracing the accompanying loneliness that would follow civilization's downfall. Like most preppers, Max prepared so that he and those he cared for could survive.

He wanted no part of the coming apocalypse. Nevertheless, whether he wanted it or not, he was ready for it.

"Done," he said out loud.

Max would have loved to sleep now. He desperately needed it, having only had a few hours of sleep the last few days of long driving and lots of physical exertion. He was exhausted, but the Kings' party was minutes away, and as exhausted as he felt, he had made a promise. Much more, living with so many worries, he needed the mental diversion and companionship.

He left by the front door to keep up appearances, just in case someone might be watching. After locking up the "beach warehouse," he stopped on the street, looking with admiration at his years of work and some of his finest preparations. He was sure no one could tell that this home was any different from any of the others on this block. He took a lot of pride in the planning, the design, and the workmanship that had gone into this house. However, worries always filled his mind with doubt and an overriding need to be careful. So, even though he had conducted this exercise what seemed like a thousand times, he once again scrutinized the house objectively, making sure that there were no breaches in his security and that no one could see the secrets within. No, he was sure. *It looks damned good.*

He started walking toward his beach home, but then another sensation stopped him cold–the sense that someone was watching him. He hesitated and then turned around, facing the beach warehouse once more. His prideful smile now erased, he looked around the street and then to other houses. He was probably just being paranoid, just second-guessing himself, but his life and the life of the Kings depended on his being careful. He searched for something out of place, someone who didn't belong. There were two different trucks he didn't recognize parked near the beginning of their block, but that was not uncommon with so many visitors to this place and a couple of houses being rented to people he didn't know. Out the corner of his eye, he sensed some movement at Judas Feinstein's bedroom window but immediately dismissed this as well. There was no one there. He was tired. The movement was in his mind.

He turned and walked through his beach house gates and into his home to clean up and relax a little. It was time to celebrate his preparedness. After this, he believed they might never again have reason to celebrate.

He was right.

18.
Prying Eyes
7:30 P.M.

Judas Feinstein was always leering at his neighbors. Plying either
his binoculars or his telescope, he searched for hours each day,
often feeding his fat jowls, but never removing his eyes from his
prey. This was his Internet. As when surfing the web, he never
knew what he was searching for until he found it--or them. But as
with any skill exercised over the years, he was expert in knowing
his neighbors' windows, terraces, and pools better than they did.
He relished invading their private lives unknowingly with his
prying eyes. His rewards were abundant, as he often found a
neighbor or two without clothes or in the middle of an argument.
Occasionally, he would catch others who believed they were
hidden on the beach, or in their driveways, or in their cars, doing
things they shouldn't. His eyes searched everywhere and
anywhere, hoping for some action.

Judas also had his favorites, those whose routines he had
memorized. He pointed his prying gaze toward his two favorite
dykes, Eve and Alice, who lived full-time in RP, three doors down
at 20. They often loved to sunbathe in the nude on their terrace,
feeling safe, while he would stare at their bodies. Of the two, the
younger--he called her Eve even though she could have been
Alice--was his more desired. Judas knew every curve and blemish
of Eve's beautiful body, often glistening in the sun from sweat and

tanning oil. If he was really lucky, he would catch them in their lovemaking.

A noise below interrupted his interlude. Looking down and to his left he recognized his strangest neighbor, Maxwell Thompson. Judas met him a couple of times and hated him from the beginning, mostly because he never told Judas what he did, and his curtains were always drawn so that Judas could never see in. *Like his business is more important than everyone else's.* He also hated Thompson because his large inland house, next door to him, had the highest terrace on their block. Not only did it obstruct his seeing summer sunrises, it also restricted him from seeing the terrace and most of the house of Max's next-door neighbor, Clydeston. Judas often wondered what kind of erotic show he was missing, especially since Clydeston always had some sort of hottie for a girlfriend. One night last year, Clydeston had brought *two* hotties home. He could see them get out of Clydeston's Ferrari convertible, but he couldn't see anything else because of his damned neighbor Thompson.

Thompson's inland house next door to him at 27 was even stranger than Thompson was, or was it even a real house? Thompson already had his beachside home at 28, so it made no sense that he maintained an inland house that no one ever stayed in and was never rented. *So, what's the deal?* Its lights would go on and off like clockwork to appear as if someone was occupying it. Nevertheless, any idiot could tell he used timers. Then there were the giant loads of supplies and strange hours. Thompson would sometimes show up at odd times with one of his two vehicles. He would park in the extra-large garage, and then disappear for hours before reemerging out the front door and walking to the beach house across the street. Sometimes, he would never be seen leaving by his front door and then magically appear outside his beachside home hours later, as if he had made himself invisible to get across the street.

Last night, he came in with his trailer full and canopied, which prevented Judas from seeing its cargo. All evening and today, he was there. Then, just now, right after sunset, he had opened up his front door, walked to the street, turned and stared at his house, and smiled like some idiot for what seemed like five minutes. Before going home, his whole demeanor had changed, and he started looking around--and then right at Judas. As if Thompson knew Judas was spying on him. But Thompson couldn't see him, he was sure of it, as he had put a special reflective film on his windows to enable his daylight peeping. Before sunset, Judas always made sure he wasn't backlit, using the Clapper, so he didn't have to move his large frame to turn off the lights. That way, someone like Thompson couldn't see him. Yet, there was Thompson staring right at him, through his window, as if saying, "I see you, asshole," through his binoculars.

Then Thompson had shaken his head, turned his back to Judas and left.

Judas put his binoculars down on the table in front of him and grabbed his Mexican cell phone. He held the number 2 key down until he heard ringing.

"*¿A qué huele carajo?*" A voice yelled out of his earpiece, which he promptly muffled by putting his oversized head against it.

"Seenyour Rodrigo? Ahhh... Esta Judas," Judas said, struggling with his broken Spanish, his flabby face turning red.

"I know who it is. What do you want?" Rodrigo shouted back in perfect English.

"Seenyour Thompson brought back another big load of something last night. I don't know what it was, because it was covered, but there was a lot of it. I think it might have been drugs or something."

"I don't pay you to think. Is that all?"

"Si... I mean yes."

"Fine, call me when you have something useful to report." With that, he hung up.

"But, should I..." Judas moved the phone away from his ear and looked at it to confirm that Rodrigo had hung up on him.

"Bloody fucking drug dealers," he yelled at his phone, slamming it down on the table in front of him. The flabby folds of his arm, absorbing the blow, swayed back and forth. His wispy white eyebrows were furrowed in fury, and the blood vessels under the pale skin of his forehead popped out.

He wished he could check out Thompson's house further and see what he was up to. However, all his windows were tinted or mirrored so that you couldn't look in them. It looked like he had security cameras, so Judas couldn't very well stick his face up against the window.

"Bloody hell," Judas shouted again.

He had other work to do. He stuck his bloodshot right eye against his telescope's sight and swung it around to the Smiths' residence at 24, who as luck would have it were barbequing in their swimsuits on their terrace. Mrs. Smith was hot and wearing a nice bikini.

Judas forgot about Thompson and stared intently through his telescope, licking his lips at what was unfolding before his eyes.

~~~

Rodrigo didn't have time for this now. He knew he would have to deal with Max soon, but he had been avoiding it for years, ever since his father, Felix "El Chorro" Menendez, had put him in charge of their Sonoran operations. Max was a friend of the family since the day he kicked their asses in the streets of Puerto Penasco when they were picking on that *maricón* Miguel. He knew Max was up to something and was probably hoarding some contraband, but he didn't want to anger his father, as much as he would like to take down Max once and for all. Maybe it would be soon. He took in the last draw of his Dos Equis and put it down loudly, purposely interrupting the only two men in the room, who were focused intently on their own beers and their game of dominos, the older one regaling the younger with bravado about his sexual exploits. Rodrigo only had two *esclavos* at the compound to check on this lead. The rest of his *ascinos* were already at their homes, ready when he needed them for something important.

"*Cabrónes*," he yelled, enjoying the fear his power created.

"*Averiguen la casa del Señor Max.* That *maricón* Judas called and said Max brought back another shipment. Park a block away, and watch what happens tonight and tomorrow and report to me. Stay in your car and wait for my call, unless you see something. If you do, report to me first. Do not engage him."

"*No hay problema*, Rodrigo," one of the two replied.

"And be careful," Rodrigo continued, "We know he has weapons and how to use them. So tread lightly, or you might end up *muertos* from your stupidity."

"*No hay problema*, Rodrigo." They spoke in unison, stood up, and left without asking another question.

19.
The Party
9:30 P.M.

"This is not science fiction, Clyde. This is fact." Max was very animated at the challenge laid out before him by Clyde, saying in so many alcohol-flavored words that he was just another "George-Noory-listening fool" who believed in any crazy scenario and that this most recent one didn't have even a remote element of truth. *Game on.*

The debate started when Clyde said he could run his whole house from his new tablet. Max said it wouldn't matter when the next big CME wiped out all his electronic toys, what would he have to show for himself?

Bill was going to enjoy this, mostly because Clyde was such a pompous SOB, who was due for a tongue-lashing. Max was just the man to do it.

"Every one hundred years, the Earth experiences massive solar storms like the one that hit in September 1859.

"The whole world as far south as Cuba witnessed auroras in the skies for several days. All telegraph communications went down. Telegraph lines exploded, raining sparks and fire on terrified witnesses, even electrocuting some. There were no other electric gadgets then and no computers with circuit boards. Nothing else for the EMPs to fry.

"Now imagine if this were to happen today. Anything that could have conducted electrical current did, because of the massive magnetic waves that pummeled the Earth then. You think your smart phones, tablets, TVs, and other useless things would survive? No, computers run everything we have now: cars, appliances, pacemakers, games. Everything we depend on runs on electricity and would be fried in an instant with a large 1859-sized EMP. Power grids would go down permanently, and would take ten to twenty or more years to replace. No power for twenty years. All sectors of society would collapse: banking, medicine, factories, transportation, farming. All wiped out. It would be the end of our world as we know it." Max had his prey cornered, and he wasn't going to let up.

Clyde was looking a little ashen. Everyone else was silent, listening intently. *This is Max at his finest,* Bill thought.

Max continued the assault.

"Worse yet, I've only mentioned a rather common solar event that happens every two to four generations. The next one will happen during this very one, while we are alive. In fact, scientists estimate better than a fifty-percent chance it will happen before your next girlfriend's boob job."

Clyde just glared at him. His girlfriend, awaking from her catatonic state, realized some attention was on her but didn't know why.

Max, smiling, continued. "But there is the potential for an event which is so much worse than this.

"Every few thousand years or so, the Earth gets pummeled by solar super storms hundreds of times worse than what it experienced in 1859. We're talking months of fire and brimstone, the likes of which the Bible talks about with the destruction of evil

Sodom and Gomorrah. Know this: when that happens, your ass is toast. You will not survive." He was speaking to all the guests now.

"But, I just may. Not because I'm smarter than any of you... aside from Clyde here." A few chuckles erupted around the room. "It's because I have planned for the end of the world. I've hedged my bets, while you, Clyde, sit on your lazy butt watching MSNBC on your satellite TV, worrying about such trivial issues as what politician sexted pictures of his lower anatomy to some young intern. I'll be ready, Clyde, when our world comes to an end. What will you do?" Max ended confidently.

"Mmmm. What about all those preparations for the coming zombie apocalypse, Max? I seem to recall a similar tone of certainty emanating from you about five years ago. How'd that work out for you?" Clyde's rebuttal was quick and damning, to be sure.

"Come on, Clyde, I vanna go now. Dis talk is boring," Clyde's very pretty Slavic-sounding girlfriend said while tugging him toward the door. "I vanna go dancing at On The Beach."

"Okay, fine. Thanks, Bill and Lisa, for the wonderful party." Clyde leaned over and kissed Lisa on her check. "Bye Sally," he waved across the room to her. "Both your women get sexier each time I see them," he said while shaking his host's hand.

They were gone just as suddenly.

Not long after everyone left, Max did his best to stay awake while Bill and Lisa cleaned up. Now would have been a good time to tell the Kings what was coming, but he was in no shape to do it. After two days of no sleep, rigorous manual labor, worry about the end of the world, and the alcohol from Bill's margaritas, Max was done in.

"Family, I need to call it a night," he said, looking somewhat pale. He arose from the loveseat in the open den and walked into the kitchen to offer his goodbyes.

"No, Uncle Max," Sally stood up from one of the kitchen bar seats and pleaded with him. "You can't go yet. I've been trying all night to speak to you about what you said to Mr. Clydeston and the solar storms we're having."

His head felt like it was about to pop like an overripe grape in the sun. He turned to her. "I'm sorry. I'm just a little too tired right now. Let's try tomorrow?" He gave Sally a hug and kiss on the cheek.

"Yeah, sure. Sleep well, Uncle Max," Sally conceded for the time being.

"Tired from the Clyde Clydeston throw-down?" Lisa couldn't help but goad him a little before he left. She handed Bill the last dish to dry, both of them standing behind the kitchen island.

"Ha. That damned Clydeston is a pretentious asshole." Max then gave his puppy dog look. "Lisa, I'm sorry if I embarrassed you. I'm just tired and shouldn't have said what I did. Especially when it's obvious in the coming da..." He stopped himself. "Truth is, I really hate that guy. What he needs is a good physical ass kicking, or better yet, a .50-cal round to the skull."

Bill was imagining Max on the roof of his house taking Clyde out from a mile away, having difficulty repressing his smile.

"Max, enough. You never embarrass me. I just thought you were a little heavy, considering the otherwise festive occasion," Lisa rebutted. "What did you mean when you said *when it's obvious*?"

"Tomorrow. Now sleep," Max said, kissing Lisa on the

check and then hugging her husband. "Thanks, Bill," he offered upon releasing him, quietly leaving by the patio door before he said anything else he shouldn't.

20.

Dr. Reid
June 28th, 2:10 A.M.
Salt Lake City, Utah

His eyes were bloodshot and tear-filled from lack of sleep and from his "goodbyes" to his daughter and grandson over the phone. He knew he would never see them again, but felt a little hope that they might make it. They lived in a very rural area in France, where his son-in-law managed a four-hundred-year-old vineyard in the Burgundy valley. They were smart and had paid attention to his warnings years ago, stocking up about four years' worth of food and water.

His wife had long since passed, and so he had no more family about whom to worry. His concerns were broader now. They were for the human race.

Carrington reviewed his report one more time before closing it and dragging it to the secure cloud-storage account they had given him several years ago when he started receiving the bulk of his funding from Cicada.

He opened his wallet and pulled out a well-creased piece of paper, folded in quarters. He opened it and smoothed it out with the palm of his right hand, holding it with the forefinger and thumb of his left. Squinting to make out the somewhat faded writing, he realized he hadn't looked at it for almost six years now. He typed in the IP address and waited for the secure website to boot.

Carrington considered his next move: the one described to him by his handlers on that fateful day he accepted their money. From what he remembered, back then, fewer than 50 people held the same instructions he did, but none had ever used them until now.

He typed in the password at the prompt and hit the "Enter" key.

The others like him gladly jumped at the money, which was substantial, simply to do what they wanted to do: their own research. Additionally, they had to report their findings periodically, and most important, one of them would announce the end of the world.

Most were like him, scientists, doctors, and researchers all in fields that studied and/or prognosticated about the end. He was sure there would be one or two astrophysicists who searched the heavens for Earth-bound asteroids or malevolent ETs, or volcanologists who waited for the tell-tale sign of a new ring of fire erupting from the Earth's fragile mantle, or surely a cacophony of microbiologists and epidemiologists watching for the newest deadly bird flu or Ebola. He tried to imagine what his fellow scientists would say when they saw that auroras would signal humanity's downfall. Would they be jealous or relieved that they were not the Paul Revere of this ensuing global apocalypse?

His fingers found the keyboard and typed in what his instructions commanded. He pressed the "Enter" key once more.

A blinking prompt instructed, "Thank you Dr. Reid. Please submit to retinal scan."

Carrington leaned forward to the special webcam attached to his monitor. A red light passed left to right and then up and down over his right eye, while he concentrated on not blinking.

"Accepted" flashed on his screen. Then, almost instantaneously, the software he, other paid prognosticators, and other benefactors of Cicada's benevolence, had loaded on their computers opened up a pulsating red warning screen that ordered "CLICK HERE."

Carrington was shocked that there was no review by some committee first. He had expected a delay of at least a few minutes, while those that oversaw the money made a decision that could affect the human race. Just like that, Carrington had put the wheels into motion. He clicked on the link, which opened the following message on his screen:

Attention! The Cicada Protocol has been initiated. You are to report immediately to The Cicada Project. The time is at hand. Your instructions have been sent to your desktop, ready to be opened and then printed. This message, your instructions, and your computer's hard-drive will self-destruct within 15 minutes, enough time to sort out your affairs. Do not forward this message to anyone. We are monitoring your computer and methods of communication.

Do not take anyone with you except your immediate family. Unfortunately, space is limited.

If you deviate from your instructions, you will be turned away from The Cicada Project.

We offer our prayers and thanks to you and your family for your commitment and for your safe travels here.

Cicada 3301

After checking his watch, Carrington did as instructed and opened the .pdf that pulsated on his desktop, then printed the three pages of instructions. Making sure that he had everything, he then opened up his bulk mail program for CMERI.

He quickly typed out his last bulletin. Doing a rapid review and correcting only one typo, he hit the "Send" button, broadcasting the bulletin only via email, afraid he would run out of time if he attempted to also post it to their website. The 24,000 people who subscribed to CMERI's email bulletins would receive this. He wondered how many of those followed his directions. Six years and millions of dollars, with the main point of getting the word out, and only 24,000 people had subscribed.

"So few," he lamented out loud.

However, a few dozen of those were reporters, many of whom had already reported his dire warnings. They would certainly report this. Few would take heed to the warning reported until it was too late. Of course, it was already too late unless you were a prepper of some sort.

Or a Mormon. He chuckled at the thought.

His computer began to make a strange noise and then he smelled smoke. Turning his wrist, he saw on the watch his wife had given to him for their twentieth anniversary that it was exactly fifteen minutes from when the message had first appeared on his screen. He slid his rolling chair back, thinking that maybe the computer would explode. Instead, it sizzled and something popped in the computer case, and then the monitor went dark.

To: Maxwell Thompson

From: bulletins@CMEResearchInstitute.org

Subject: A CARRINGTON EVENT IS COMING!

CME Research Institute
www.CMEResearchInstitute.org

BULLETIN

28 June

A CARRINGTON EVENT IS COMING!

A large CME, preceded by ten smaller CMEs, came into contact with our atmosphere 46 minutes ago. The fullness of its effects is not yet known, but we expect considerable damage to many areas, especially Polar Regions which are less protected by the magnetosphere (the Earth's electromagnetic shield).

The effects of the cascading CMEs over the last few days are well known now. However, lesser known is that with each CME, the magnetosphere is being worn down (the best way we can explain it). It appears that this continual diminishment is progressive, allowing greater amounts of solar radiation to break through our ionosphere from each subsequent solar storm. We expect a tripling or quadrupling of the sun's radiation worldwide over the next few days or weeks. The new normal now appears to be multiple hourly coronal mass eruptions, which will further disrupt the magnetosphere. Besides the ensuing deleterious effects to our bodies (e.g. cellular degeneration and malignancies such as carcinoma), the additional solar radiation will heat up our planet, causing the following: polar icecap melting and ensuing flooding of all coastal lands; widespread fires; and terrestrial reduction of plant and animal life, and therefore a world-wide decline of food sources.

The news we bring is far worse. Our data indicates a colossal coronal mass ejection has erupted and we estimate the bulk of plasma and ensuing electromagnetic waves will hit Earth within 24 hours or less.

This solar storm is the one we all feared and we have tried to warn everyone about.

Unfortunately, we cannot do much to help you. Even if we had recommended that you stock up on supplies, short of a warehouse full of food, it will not be enough. This coming CME will destroy all electrical power, taking down all utilities, infrastructure, and communications. We expect all electronics, other than the most hardened, to be destroyed by the ensuing inductive electromagnetic waves. Across the entire planet, all computers and the Internet will be gone by tomorrow.

We will continue to monitor this situation and maintain our site (www.CMEResearchInstitute.org). However, when what we are calling The Event occurs, there will be no way to connect to our systems, which we know will eventually go down like all others.

Our sincere hope is that some of you reading this, especially those who have already prepared for this, will survive. We pray for you our readers, for our country, and for humanity.

Dr. Carrington Reid, Founder
CME Research Institute

21.
Putting It All Together
5:05 A.M.
Rocky Point, Mexico

Sally received 9827 pluses and over 2500 comments on her post two days ago. This alone wasn't what unnerved her, as she had had many great posts that her community of followers would get excited about, some even rising to the level of "What's Hot," the term Google uses to describe posts which are going viral and are then seen by every subscriber of Google+. It wasn't even the sheer number of direct reports by people who were witnessing or were affected by the solar flares she was reporting.

She wasn't sure how they were finding her post and why it tapped something in so many, but it had. From all over the globe, people were talking about the strange auroras they had witnessed or the destruction in Asia, Northern Europe, and Alaska.

She had also used the Twitter hashtag of #solarevent; others followed suit, causing her computer and/or phone to ping almost every second with continual reports, some of which she shared on Google Plus.

Even her assistant, Brian, was deep into the comments. As one of the managers of her page, he could offer more, including additional images that were being sent by witnesses.

What made her most anxious were two specific posts.

First was from someone claiming to work for NASA. He said that the ISS was "dead in the sky," literally fried by the solar storm that was currently wreaking havoc with Earth's magnetosphere. He added that what they had witnessed was only going to be followed by something much worse, but didn't elaborate, saying that he was already breaking the law by posting what he had.

The second post, from yesterday, was from a Dr. Carrington Reid. The same Carrington Reid was featured in the article she pointed to in her post, *Noted Solar Physicist Predicts a Global Apocalypse*. He said that we have gone through this all before, something called a Carrington Event; she wondered if it was named after him or vice versa. Further, he said, "There is a 90% chance of a solar eruption, equal to or worse than the Carrington event with a coronal mass ejection so massive that when it hits the Earth sometime within two days, all our power will go down and all of our electronic devices will be destroyed or rendered useless." That we would be "literally brought back to the Stone Age." He then offered his web address (CMEResearchInstitute.org), and that was it.

Sally and Brian tried to engage further with both "John Smith of NASA" and the less anonymous "Dr. Reid," but neither replied. Emails and calls to Dr. Reid were unanswered.

She pulled up CME Research Institute's website (or CMERI as they liked to refer to themselves), and read about the Carrington Event that occurred in 1859. She read further about the dire warnings and posts of these CMEs occurring all the time. Then she downloaded a free survival book from their website, *The Solar Apocalypse Survival Guide*, even though it sounded a little too much like what would be found on one of those websites that catered to the crazies. *Perhaps they aren't too crazy*, she thought.

Then it all hit her: realization of what Max had been saying at the party, why he had her dad build that safe room for them and their electronics, and what was about to come... to everyone.

22.
Coffee
9:10 A.M.
Clear Lake, Michigan

Darla took a sip from her coffee and then continued. "No, Google Plus is a much better social platform than Twitter and certainly Facebook. All your posts are searchable, whereas they are not on Facebook."

"Yeah, but it's a digital wasteland," Steve refuted as gently as he could. "They only have a half a billion users."

"ONLY? Really? Actually, it's just over one billion, and it was built in only a couple of years versus over a decade for Facebook. Besides, FB is for silly exercises like poking and friending, G+ is for serious people."

"I don't suppose your exuberance has anything to do with your sister Sally making a living off it?" *Oops, the cat is out of the bag now*, he thought.

"How…"

"Okay, I admit it. I'm one of Sally's followers." Steve then added bashfully, "She's a good writer, and well, I was curious when I saw the name."

"Should I be jealous that you followed my sister before me?" She played with him.

"I couldn't even find your profile… I--"

"I'm just playing with you. I'm glad you looked for me." Her face radiated a full smile.

"Me too." Steve grinned back.

They sat silent for a long, comfortable moment, without any awkwardness, just enjoying where their newfound relationship was going.

Darla broke the silence first. "So tell me. Where are you and your dad flying, and why all the mystery?"

Steve proceeded to tell her all about Cicada, including showing her the GPS location on his phone. His phone interrupted, pinging with an incoming text.

"Sorry," he glanced at the screen. "I've really gotta go. I actually have to do a little work before we head out tonight." He reached into his pocket and pulled out something, laying it on the table.

"What is this?" she asked, puzzled.

"You gave me a little sand dollar from when you went to Mexico. I had it covered in silver and made it into a necklace... Ah, it's for you."

"I remember that. Wait, you've been planning this for a while."

"Is it too much? Am I starting to scare you? You know--"

She kissed him this time, long and slow.

She gradually withdrew, and when she opened her eyes, he said with a grin, "I love kissing you."

"Me too. We need to continue this, although I don't know when."

His phone chirped again, pulling him away. "Me neither, but I promise you, we will again soon."

23.
The Teacher
7:15 P.M.
Joliet, Illinois

The crowds are ginormous, Thomas thought. Far bigger and different from any other revival he had ever seen. They all came to see, to hear, and for some, to be healed by the Teacher. "The press," he told Thomas, "fanned the flames of the embers I already ignited in the hearts of men." Thomas didn't exactly know what that meant, but it felt true. And on fire was right, because every night they did a gathering, the crowds got bigger. Now the Teacher was, as his daddy would have said, "hotter than a whorehouse on dollar night."

It started, at least for Thomas, outside Charleston, but then grew as the Teacher and his group of followers traveled the rural highways from West Virginia, through Ohio, then Indiana, and now Illinois, in the southern rural suburbs of Chicago, always working their way west. Now, it was Joliet. With each town, the crowds grew. Today, hours before the big event, there were over one thousand people. Many had attended on a previous night, but today, they brought family members, who probably had told their loved ones they were "full of bunk" after hearing their testimony.

When he first met the Teacher, Thomas had been like many of them, sitting there waiting, hurting on the inside. He was unemployed after working in the mines for years. Then, his government checks ran out and his bitch of a wife kicked him out.

Let her take care of those snot nose shits herself, he thought.

While he was thumbing for a ride to Columbus, where he heard his second cousin's boss might have a job for him, somebody handed him a flyer. He couldn't read so he asked, "What is this bullshit?" The guy told him, all happy, "Come for free and you will be saved. There's a map on the back." He never made it to Columbus.

Thomas had seen lots of preachers in his day, but this one was different. The man, whom everyone called Teacher and no other name, was amazing. Thomas went to one gathering--the Teacher didn't like calling them revivals--and came out like he was drunk, his mind all twisted up. He had to go again. The second night, Thomas touched the Teacher and something happened he couldn't explain. The Teacher felt him touch his clothes and turned to him, giving him a big smile and staring into his brain, as if he could read his thoughts. He said, "Thomas, your worries are few. Lift up your infirmities unto me." The Teacher grabbed his hand and said something, and it was as if he was filled with electricity. Then, he felt peace. His mind was quiet. Before he looked up, the Teacher was already several people behind him.

On the third gathering he went to, there was a miracle. "It was no parlor tricks like those done by most big tent revival healers, or like you would see at the fair," he would tell others. Those false preachers always reminded him of the movie his bitch of a wife loved, the one starring Steve Martin who played the huckster preacher, using slight-of-hand deceptions to cheat hard-working farmers out of their money. The Teacher was different. He performed real miracles.

Thomas thought back to when a man known by the whole town to have been born blind at birth approached the stage. The Teacher walked up to him and asked him what he wanted, and the blind man fell to his knees and said, "If you are willing, Teacher, heal me."

The Teacher said, "Arise, you are cleansed. Now, go tell the world."

The man stood up and turned to the faces in the crowd, who were silent, anticipating. The blind man opened his eyes. Thomas could see him clear as day. The milky color in his pupils was gone, replaced with dark eyes that stared in shock at the crowds, then the ceiling of the tent, and then his hands. His mouth opened but he spoke no words.

He didn't need to say nothing. We all knew what he felt.

Tears ran down his cheeks. It was like a high-school football game when the home team scores at the last second to win. Everyone went nuts.

On the fourth night, when the Teacher passed by, he turned again and said right at him, "Follow me, Thomas." He had been with him since then, doing odd jobs and trying to learn.

After the Teacher made the blind man see, the press started showing up. Their headlines asked the question a lot of people had on their minds and lips. "Was this Jesus' Second Coming?" Thomas didn't know any of this, and didn't care. He was there because the Teacher asked him to follow, and he didn't think he could say no.

24.
Quiet Before the Storm
6:30 P.M.
Rocky Point, Mexico

Max's computer slept like its owner, quietly.

His phone's battery was dead and recharging. Similarly, his body and mind were unconsciously cocooned, recharging in REM sleep. His rhythmic breathing spoke of a peace he had found nowhere else the last couple of days. While a few others around the world--those who were paying attention to the signs above-- were frantically preparing for the end, Max had done his work long before others even realized what was happening. Max had earned his rest. So now, he slept.

When Max had returned from the King's party last night, he was so exhausted he couldn't even bother removing his clothes before flopping onto his bed. Sometime in the night he managed to wiggle out of his boots; the rest of him lay in a discarded heap, fully clothed and quietly breathing, on his back. He was even too tired to dream.

That day, Max slept through everything. His exhaustion consumed him. He slept through the early morning, not even stirring when several seagulls somehow became confused in flight and hit the side of his house, a few so hard they broke their necks, their bodies coming to rest upon his deck.

Then in the late morning, he slept through Sally vigorously knocking on his patio door, seeking answers to her questions.

Then, in the early afternoon hours, a pelican ran into his satellite dish, killing itself and his satellite dish simultaneously. The pelican's carcass slid down a course of solar panels before crashing through a glass table on the patio, and coming to rest in a heap of glass, feathers, and blood. The dish dangled over the side of his bedroom wall, tethered by its thick black coaxial cable. Perhaps it was the noise, or perhaps he was done sleeping on his back, but Max rolled over onto his stomach and slept some more.

He even slept through the quiet of sunset, its eerie light calling to him, unheard.

Before finally being awakened by bad dreams and the pounding on his door, he had slept a total of seventeen hours.

25.
Miracles
8:30 P.M.
Joliet Illinois

The stadium floodlights kicked on, working their soft orange rays into the shadows of dusk, pushing back the inevitable darkness. It was late, but no one cared. The Joliet High School Hornets football stadium had never seen a crowd this big, including the night they won state. Throngs of eager people filled the stands, the bleachers, and all grassy areas on the field. Some were even on top of their cars in the parking lot, and two sat precariously upon one of the goal posts. All were quietly listening to the Teacher.

He stood on a slightly elevated platform that made him look that much taller. He was a manifestation built up by word of mouth, fueled by an overzealous media and buttressed by his own charismatic presence. The Teacher was educating the crowd about judgment day. It was one of his favorite topics, one he spoke of a lot recently.

"This know also, that in the last days perilous times shall come. And you will hear of wars and rumors of wars. See that you are not alarmed, for this must take place. For nation will rise against nation, and kingdom against kingdom, and there will be famines and earthquakes in various places. All these are but the beginning of the birth pains." He paused for impact.

"Lawlessness will increase and the love of many will grow cold, but the one who endures to the end will be saved."

The stadium lights started to flicker.

"For then there will be great tribulation, such as has not been from the beginning of the world until now, and never will be." His voice rose in strength for emphasis.

The lights flickered again, this time followed by a few gasps from some in the crowd.

"Immediately after the tribulation of these days, the world will be plunged into darkness."

~~~

Only a few miles away, the Dresden Nuclear Power Plant was a buzz of activity. From the air, the workers running around the plant would have looked like ants evading a large predator. The predator invading Dresden was silent and unseen, and far more deadly than any attacker imagined by the Nuclear Power Plant Preparedness Plan.

Induced currents from a moderate sized CME currently working its way to Earth built up along power lines leading to the station's main transformers. To protect itself, when current levels reached 110% above baseline, the power plant's system disconnected itself from the grid, in essence shutting itself down from power production. Unfortunately, tonight was also an unusually warm summer night in Chicagoland, which was pulling more than its fair share of energy from the grid. The Joliet Power Station, on the NERC's watch list for not having proper shielding around its transformers, was already struggling to keep up with normal power demands. The same CME-induced currents that were playing havoc at Dresden started to cause cascading circuit overloads at Joliet. When Dresden shut down, Joliet's transformers failed.

~~~

The lights went out at Joliet High School stadium, followed by the school's lights, followed by the streetlights, followed by the AM/PM Mini Mart a block away. It was a blackout.

The Teacher paused, and now many more murmured and whispered. He flicked the microphone on/off switch a couple of times to verify it was not working, confirming its power appeared to be cut off too. He turned and found Thomas, already anticipating what Teacher might need, handing him a bullhorn, already turned on.

He continued, "And there will be terrors and great signs from heaven."

The murmur grew louder. A dozen or so fingers were thrust into the air, pointing to the east, then a few more, and then still more, until everyone was looking to the eastern horizon, which was awash in undulating green clouds. The pulsating auroras rolled in like storm clouds, but far more sinewy and fragile looking, which didn't at all diminish their ominous presence. A few people stood up, frightened by the sight before them, as the Teacher had just prophesied. In their fear, they were no longer paying attention, tripping over others who were transfixed by the heavenly miracle they were witnessing.

One of the stadium's transformers connected to a light pole on the 20-yard line exploded. A gushing arch of sparks fanned out and rained down on the crowd sitting and standing below. The panic bubbled up through the multitude, beginning with those being covered by burning debris and then spreading out. A woman's scream sliced through the commotion, her hair having caught fire from the transformer's sparks. Terror fueled her voice and legs. Those around her joined in, now accompanying her shrieking and erratic motion, until it seemed a mass of people were rolling into the field rather than toward the exits.

Another transformer blew. This one was on the opposite end of the field by the 30-yard line. These sparks ignited a powder keg of terror. Most of the whole crowd at once attempted to flee, many falling over each other, some getting trampled to death. Only moments ago, the field had been in rapture over the Teacher's words and his promised specter of miracles. Now it was a witness to hell on Earth.

The Teacher stood resolutely on his dais, the bullhorn dangling from the cord around his wrist, and both arms outstretched at his sides. He watched intently as this sea of people ran in all directions simultaneously, their fears pushing aside any logical thinking. He slowly raised his arms skyward, as if beckoning the heavens. His face, without emotion, was composed in purposeful determination. He considered what it must have been like for Moses when he parted the seas. Only this prophet was parting a sea of people so as to separate the wheat from the chaff, or the strong from the weak. He was in command. He was the prophet of this time.

It was his time.

26.

Preflight
10:50 P.M.
Jackson County, Michigan

John and Steve Parkington arrived at the Jackson County Airport - Reynolds Field at just before 11 p.m. Steve ran into the airport restaurant to use the facilities, knowing it was going to be a while before the next rest stop, while John went to the airport manager's office to drop off their flight plan. They met at Hangar 119 and opened the door to reveal John's favorite toy, a blue-and-red striped 1982 Cessna 340A. Although he didn't need to, John had justified the purchase for business because he often traveled around the state, especially to Detroit, and sometimes across the lake to Chicago. Really, John had just bought the plane for fun. It was in sorry shape when he purchased it (or stole it), having sat unused in a field for a decade. After a year of overhauling the engine, replacing much of the avionics, reupholstering it with leather, and repainting it with his company's colors, John had a practically new plane.

While John went through his pre-flight checklist, Steve was getting weather reports all the way to Denver on his phone. Most pilots never flew at this time, even those who were instrument rated, still preferring to fly by the light of day. John loved flying at night, among the stars; he was very familiar with this route, having made this very same flight six times now. Everything looked good and they were ready to go. With a little tailwind, they should reach

Denver by sunrise at five.

"Jackson Tower, this is Cessna Charlie-George-Boy-two-two-six requesting permission to take off."

"Cessna two-two-six, be advised, Chicago O'Hare reports communications problems. Traffic is heavy in their neighborhood. Otherwise, Cessna two-two-six, you are cleared for take-off on runway three-two. Have a safe trip, John."

"Thanks, Peter, Cessna two-two-six out."

John looked at Steve, who was lost in a happy thought, smiling to himself.

"You ready?" he asked, interrupting his thoughts.

"Engage, Number One," Steve answered, thrusting his hand forward and mimicking his most favored TV series," Star Trek: Next Generation," even though it hadn't been on since he was very young.

John throttled the engines. The twin turbo props came alive in an instant, moving the airplane forward at a rapidly increasing rate. In twenty seconds, they reached 105 miles per hour. John pulled back on the wheel and they were airborne. The plane steadily accelerated, disregarding the pull of gravity. Within a few minutes, they flew over their family home and the lake they both so enjoyed. Ahead of them was an adventure that would test their intellectual and physical limits. Behind them was the home they had known for most of their lives--one they would never see again.

27.
Prelude to Armageddon
8:55 P.M.
Rocky Point, Mexico

They walked barefooted, hand in hand on the littoral area of the beach where the sand was flat, solid, and packed enough that walking wasn't difficult. The sun, already set, still provided enough light for them to avoid the occasional rock or coral. The soft afternoon waves of the low tide, not yet moving back inland, gently brushed the sand forward and back only a few steps from their feet. Both Bill and Lisa walked in anxious silence, lost in their own thoughts.

Lisa was apprehensive about Darla and Danny. They were flying late tonight, getting into Rocky Point Airport tomorrow morning on a puddle jumper. They would be doing lots of driving from Bill's father's house in Michigan and then lots of flying. She trusted Dar, who had a clear head, but was worried just the same about them leaving so late. She was always worried about Danny and his asthma. She said a little prayer to herself to calm her nerves.

Bill considered more deeply what Max had shared with him, along with Sally's frantic revelations about her Internet findings this morning. He asked her to not share them with Lisa until Max could verify them. It was still somewhat surreal that Max had built his house to protect against... from what, exactly, Bill didn't know. Then, Max stocked up with enough guns, ammo, and supplies for the end of the world. He never really gave Max's apocalyptic prognostications much thought, until now. He never doubted his sincerity or seriousness, but he never considered tangible the potential threats Max obviously lost sleep over. After being shown the secret office and gun, he first wondered if his friend was seriously off-the-reservation crazy or if the source of his worries was real. He so wanted to tell Lisa but was sure she would be terrified by most of it. No wonder Max didn't want to discuss solar flares and the "big one" that was about to hit them with Sally. Now, considering all the pieces, together the puzzle seemed clear. With it came fear.

Bill tried to consider anything that could rebut the reasons for Max's and now Sally's worries. *It just couldn't be--*

His body was jerked backward, his hand being pulled by Lisa, who had stopped rigid in her tracks. Bill stopped, too, and looked back at his wife, who was staring toward the port in the westerly direction they were walking. Her face was contorted in a mask of wonderment and awe. He didn't ask but turned in the direction she was looking, his question answered immediately.

On the westernmost edge of the sky, a small, single, green, ribbon-shaped cloud hung suspended, followed by another, and then another. Like a tsunami of green wispy clouds, the sight poured toward them from the horizon.

The same clouds elicited entirely different emotions in each of the Kings. Lisa thought the clouds were beautiful, even if they were unique. Bill, on the other hand, was terrified. "We need to go tell Max immediately," he said, pulling his wife away from the sight, and they both started jogging toward Max's home.

28.
The Foretelling
9:05 P.M.

The loud banging finally woke Max from a vivid dream of death and destruction.

In his dream, he was on a train with many passengers, all content and going about their business, unaware of what lay ahead. However, he knew that less than a mile ahead of them a bridge they were supposed to cross was out. If they didn't stop the train before this bridge, they would all plunge into the canyon below to their deaths. The canyon was so deep that from its bowels erupted the actual fires of hell. He could see in his mind's eye the fire erupting from lower levels in the canyon. And they were headed right for it.

He had to warn everyone and he had to stop the train, and he knew he was the only one who could do it. Desperately, Max tried to warn every passenger on the train about their impending doom, but for some reason, he could not speak; he was rendered mute. No matter how hard he tried to speak, the words would not come out of his mouth. He tried to point and to pantomime his warning, anything to show he was serious, but everyone ignored him.

He was completely panicked now. If he could only speak, people would know what he knew. However, they were all playing with their phones, and tablets, and laptops, oblivious to the fate that awaited them. Then he realized he couldn't even breathe. He tried to take in air, but he was unable. The lack of oxygen made him dizzy. He stumbled to his knees. No one looked his way, or even gave him notice, as if he were invisible.

To draw attention, he tried to beat on a seat in front of him with his fists. The knocking sound of his fists on the metal frame barely pierced the din of the idle chatter around him. He tried again, this time with all his strength, making more sound, but not enough. Shockwaves of pain started pulsating through his hands, wrists, and arms.

He looked up and could now clearly see the fire out the windows on both sides of them. Its flickering light reflected off the inside windows and ceiling of the train, a strange mixture of red and green. The passengers were still oblivious to him, the fire and light around them and their pending doom. They were only interested in their texting, game playing, and in whatever else they were doing on their electronic devices.

It won't be long now, he thought. It was inevitable. He would die and so would everyone else on this train.

Gasping for air, he felt faint. He banged on the seat again, this time with little authority. The train car swirled around him. He was suffocating. Out of focus…

Max sat up in bed, his forehead and armpits drenched in sweat. He gulped deep breaths of air, relishing the feeling. His heart was racing, beating heavily in his chest, but it started slowing as he realized it was only a dream. He pushed aside the panic that still wanted to hold on.

Taking another breath, he started to relax, before recognizing that his bedroom had a weird glow. An eerie green luminescence invaded through the gaps of the closed blinds on both his bedroom window and sliding glass door. The panicky feeling still had a grip on him.

There was knocking on the metal frame of the sliding glass door. A muffled voice yelled out, "Max, please get out here. You have to see this."

It was Bill.

The knocking and voice were much louder than he would have liked. Each rap on the door felt like an icepick being pushed into his head. The pain was horrible. He felt nauseated. He was still hung over.

What happened? He remembered telling off that miserable prick Clyde, saying way too much about his prepping, consuming way too many mango margaritas, and excusing himself and going right to bed. Do not pass go. Do not collect $200. "Should have taken some aspirin," he said groggily to no one while carefully holding his head. He looked at his alarm clock for some reference. It read 9:10. "Is that a.m. or p.m.?" he asked it. His head pounded some more.

"Max, are you there?" Bill continued to pound his door.

Max swung his legs over the bed with much effort and stood up. The room spun, but he steadied himself on his nightstand, still knocking something over in the process. He took one step, then two, tripping over his boots, steadying himself on the wall. He drew the vertical blinds all the way open and took a step back.

What he witnessed seemed as surreal as his dream, as if this were all still part of it. But sobering reality hit him instantly. He knew this was real. The night sky was ablaze in what looked like a green fire.

"Bill, Lisa." He unlatched the door and slid it open. "Holy Christ, Bill, how long has this been going on?" Max asked as he stepped onto his patio. Bill was standing a few steps in front of him, head craned upward toward the green, pulsating sky.

Bill turned to him, his face somewhat contorted in fear. "What is this? Is this the CME you told us about? Are we in trouble?"

"I don't know, Bill, but it looks bad." Max noticed he was resting against--more like holding himself up with--one of the pillars of his patio.

This was an aurora, he was sure of it. Like waves of water in the ocean, but instead of foamy white waves, the sky was filled with waves of green and some wisps of red. From what he read, Mexico had never had an aurora, so it had to be a CME. But where were the explosions? A CME as large as this one was, which was making auroras as far south as Mexico, should be damaging the power grid and shorting out everything electric. However, he could see his lights were still on, and so were the others on the beach.

"What the hell is going on?" Max yelled out.

29.
More Bad News
9:15 P.M.

Max gave Bill, Lisa, and Sally specific instructions, trying his best not to scare them too badly, since hysterics weren't going to help any of them. He followed his own advice, first gathering up any stray electronic devices and placing them in his protected office/workshop. He left the flat screen TVs untouched in the living room and bedrooms, along with a few other electronics, such as alarm clocks also for show, so that anyone who entered his home wouldn't wonder if he had known something before they did.

When he felt satisfied that he had gathered everything important, he closed himself in his secret office/workshop and turned on his computer and phone, which was plugged in and fully charged, since it had run out of juice before returning to Puerto Penasco. Both beeped, letting their owner know they were waking up from their long slumber.

Then, while standing over his desk thinking about what he needed to do next, it occurred to him that he didn't have any other weapons in the beach warehouse. That was just plain stupid. If they had to make a stand there, they would need far more than the one sniper rifle. He had a crate of new military-issue M4 rifles resting unopened by the far wall, one of two he had spirited across the border; the other went to El Gordo's men as payment for smuggling both. The stamp of El Gordo's Mexican shipping company was prominently displayed, which told any handlers, "Touch but do not open."

He dragged it across the concrete floor to the center island workbench and turned on the workbench light directly overhead. Grabbing a crowbar, he pried the top of the crate off, its nails crying out loudly and releasing a gun-oil smell that he found satisfying. Max removed one of the M4s. Pulling the charging handle, he examined the ejection port in the upper receiver to make sure it was empty, while pointing the front of the barrel at the light to make sure there were no obstructions. He then examined the sights. Reaching into the crate, he grabbed an empty magazine and fed it into the rifle, hearing the desired *click* sound; he released the bolt, aimed, and pulled the trigger. This generated a different clicking sound. Satisfied with his dry fire test, he released the magazine, letting it drop a few inches from the rifle into his hand. *Check*, he said mentally, placing both on the workbench.

He grabbed three other M4s and seven other magazines and placed them next to the first rifle. Then, after replacing the top to the crate, he dragged it back to the far wall, returning with an ammo can filled with the .223 rounds needed to feed his hungry dogs of war. He loaded each brand new 30-round magazine, feeding a loaded magazine into each empty weapon and placing the spares beside them. "Now, a few side arms," he said out loud, unaware that his webcam light had been on for the last few minutes.

~~~

A few miles away

The two men sat in a dark room only a few minutes' walk from Max's home. "Idiot. You forgot to turn the light off," the larger of the two said.

The smaller man typed a few key strokes, and the program they were using indicated Señor Max's webcam would now appear to be off.

"Look at that, the boxes of ammo on the bench and all the weapons, *esé*. *Mira*, there's El Gordo's stamp. Señor Max is moving guns for El Gordo now." The bigger man pointed at the 30" computer screen showing the bounty that awaited their taking. A smile, stained and encrusted with yesterday's burrito, peeked out of his black mustache and beard. He had been watching Max for a while, but this new computer genius, who told them they could turn on Señor Max's web camera remotely, had proven a wise investment by his boss. They now knew what he was hiding in his beach house--and that he was working for their enemy.

"Better tell Rodrigo what we found."

30.

Fear of Flying
11:25 P.M.
Somewhere in Indiana

Darla raced to get to O'Hare in time. Each time the traffic would slow down, she cursed under her breath so that Danny wouldn't hear. "Why is there even traffic at this time of night?" she yelled at unknowing drivers ahead of her.

Normally, she would take 12 to I94 all the way through Chicago to the Kennedy to the airport. An easy two hours, maybe three with traffic. However, it had been one thing after another. First, she left later than she wanted. Then, she had to find gas and couldn't locate an open station because of the late hour. Then, she was talked into taking Elm Valley Road so she could drop off something for Mammie's friend, but there was some sort of a tractor accident on the road. If these issues weren't enough, the traffic was bumper-to-bumper in Gary and it was like *eleven fricking p.m.*, when the highways should be empty. Finally, to top it all off, they were having a very rare aurora display in the sky, which was drawing drivers' attention away from their driving to the sky and slowing the traffic down even more. Bottom line, as her sister liked to say, she was seriously late. She even texted Stacy to let her know they would have to see each other again at the gate. It was still amazing that they ended up on the same flight together with a couple of additional friends as well, at least through Dallas. What were the chances?

Now, how to avoid missing our flight? Besides the pain of having to reschedule, and maybe missing their connection to RP, she didn't want to let Stacy and her family down. *Dammit, why didn't I leave earlier?* Stacy was so nervous about flying and had been overly excited when told they were sharing the same plane. Stacy would have a hand to hold, assuming she could convince the seat holder next to her to switch seats... *If I can even make the flight.*

"Dammit," she yelled at the group of cars that had just slowed down to a crawl in front of her. "Sorry, Danny, my bad at saying that."

Danny smiled at his sister, who never said bad words.

"Your sister is sooooo fricking stupid." Darla castigated herself.

~~~

Rocky Point, Mexico

Max's phone buzzed where it sat, announcing a call, but not audibly because its ringer was silenced. He halted his march back from his largest gun cabinet, already having set five Glocks and 2000 rounds of .45 ammo on his bench, beside the rifles and extra magazines. All were ready for transport to the beach warehouse. His phone buzzed again. He picked it up seeing no picture to reveal the caller, just the letters "L.H.O." El Gordo was calling him directly, which never happened, as El Gordo always had his henchmen contact him when he wanted something. "Now what?" Mumbling and sliding his finger across the screen, Max said, "*Bueno*, Señor Luis. What can I do for you?" His tone was respectful.

"*Bueno*, Señor Max. I am calling you as a favor. Rodrigo knows what is in those boxes we helped you with," El Gordo said very cryptically, knowing the Mexican government was probably listening. Max glared at the half-opened crate by the wall, still listening. "He has control of your webcam and can see inside of your house. So--" Max jerked his head to his left, away from the phone to his largest computer screen and the webcam resting above, *pointing directly at him.* The light wasn't on, but he read that once you had control of someone's webcam, it was easy to turn the light off. "...open the box in front of the camera and be careful."

"*Chingado,*" erupted the Mexican profanity from Max's lips before he could stop it. "*Con permiso,* Señor Luis. It is too late."

"Am sorry to hear that, my friend. I must protect my investment then. Do not leave your house. I have two men in front, watching you now. I will call again soon." With that, El Gordo hung up.

Completely unnerved, Max nearly slammed the phone onto the desk.

His computer emitted some sort of warning tone, unlike any of its normal announcements. He shakily walked over, first grabbing the violating webcam cord and pulling it out of the computer. He focused on the screen and recognized the warning he never wanted to see. "*Chingado,*" he said once again, vocalizing his dread while tossing the dead webcam away from him. It skidded across the floor, coming to a rest up against the same crate of guns it had been so interested in earlier.

Grabbing his mouse, he clicked the large "CLICK HERE" below the red pulsating warning, knowing what would come next. "Attention! The Cicada Protocol has been initiated..." Max dropped into his leather work chair. He had no time to lose now. He knew what the rest said. Hell, he had written the first protocol message, and he doubted it had changed that much.

But the information wasn't for him; it was for the Kings.

So, he played along, opening the message, instructions, and map and printing them. After making sure all three pages printed, he reached under his desk beside where his soon-to-be-dead computer currently sat. He grabbed a satchel and placed it reverently on his desk. He blew on the top, disturbing a thin layer of dust. Opening the satchel, he reached in and grabbed the wrapped package and pulled it out. It looked just as he left it a few years ago. Quickly undoing the flaps of the package, he opened the book it had sheltered, admiring it for just a moment, and then slipped the printed pages into it. He wrapped it up and placed it back in the satchel, leaving it there for the moment.

"Time for that Mission Impossible thing," he announced. He reached down, yanked the cords out of the computer, and dragged the computer case to the middle of the floor, its little rubber feet trying to hold onto its position, screeching their discontent.

He opened a recently purchased laptop, booted it, and booted the word processing program. A message he had never seen before popped open. It said, "Your computer has been infected with the Zombie Computer Virus. It will now eat itself and all of your other computers…"

A smirk broke out on his lips. "Sally? Dammit. I wish I could enjoy this." He remembered her borrowing his laptop the last time she was here at the house to install some new software she had gotten for free. "Zombie virus?" He shook his head once more.

The smile ebbed as he refocused on the job at hand. Closing the window on the fake program, he chose his "From the Desk of…" template and started to write, "To my family (William, Lisa & Sally)…"

The computer in the middle of his concrete floor began emitting a hissing sound, mimicking the deflating mood he felt as he continued to write. A small cloud of smoke, no more than a puff or two from a good cigar, exhaled out of the back, signaling his trusty computer's exit from this world.

Turning away from the show, Max finished his letter and printed it out. He reread it to make sure it said what he wanted it to say, scratching the nickname they all used rather than his initials on the bottom – his normal method of signing to make it "official." Then he placed the letter on top of the wrapped package, slipped both into the satchel, and then set it in its normal resting place under the desk.

"What am I forgetting?" he asked his laptop before closing it. He spun 90 degrees in his chair to look out into his workshop, hoping something would stand out.

He stared first at his dead computer, close to a small organized pile of things heaped on the floor, taken from other parts of the house. He hoped Bill had a similar pile in his "protected" room. A couple of Mexican cell phones, a watch, a few solid metal sculptures, his favorite alarm clock--anything with value that was electronic or had a large amount of metal or other conductive material.

"It should be any time now." He blew out a large breath. A large weight was bearing down on him. In addition to the end of the world occurring any moment, which was enough for anyone, he understood it was a matter of minutes or hours before one or both of the two drug lords he knew considered him too much of a liability. He just hoped that he'd thought through this scenario well enough to protect his best friend, his family, and with a little luck, himself.

So intent was he that he didn't even notice his muted phone was attempting to give him other warnings.

~~~

O'Hare Airport

Stacy Jenkin's face crinkled into a smile, the recognition of her phone speaking to her, alone as she was in a sea of people at the airport. Five passengers from the next flight sat behind her at the gate's waiting area, all engaged with their devices, while also disconnected from everyone else they were sitting with. Stacy stood outside the area in the path of hurried travelers, who breezed by her as if she didn't exist. She watched intently for any sign of her friends.

She brought her phone up to her face, trying to see if it was Dar calling or texting, but it was only a spam email: "You may qualify for low priced term insurance. Get a quote now before..." She ignored the rest, clicking the phone's hibernate button. Her face and shoulders sagged in disappointment.

She expectantly scanned the throngs of people coming at her from all directions. Dar had texted her an hour ago saying that she was running late and they'd see her at the gate. But Stacy's subsequent texts went unanswered. She tried calling Dar, too, but she never picked up. "Where are you, Dar? I need you," she said to the crowd, who never acknowledged her pleas. The thought of flying without Dar to hold her hand brought her close to panicking. She wasn't sure how she was going to fly, and had even considered cancelling, but when Dar had said she would be on the same flight, Stacy had been ecstatic.

"Last call for flight three-six-three to Dallas."

"Oh no. What am I supposed to do now? Maybe I can get a later flight." She muttered to herself in quiet panic.

"Stacy Jenkins, is that you?" An out-of-breath voice reached her, and a familiar form emerged from the crowds in front of her, dragging a little boy behind.

A big grin broke out on Stacy's lips. "Thank God."

31.
ISS Dead to the World
June 29, 05:20 G.M.T.
In orbit, over Australia

From a porthole, R.T. glared at the auroras blanketing the Earth below, arms crossed tight to his chest. Those damned CMEs ruined everything, dooming his last mission in space. If it was possible to hate something inanimate and ethereal, he did. The ISS had been dark for almost 24 hours now. He and the crew had tried everything they could think of to jumpstart their systems, but nothing worked. There was no help for them below, as the Earth had its own problems now. R.T. knew they were hours away from death if they did nothing further. The only unknown was how death would come. Would they freeze to death, run out of oxygen, or burn in a fire? His money was on freezing to death. For warmth, each wore every layer of clothing brought on board: perhaps four total, and their suits, without helmets. Regardless, deprived of any electronics, there was no way to heat what was left of the ISS.

What else could they do? EMPs from the sun's CMEs had taken out their communications and then fried everything, including all their other electronics, in spite of their shielding. R.T. figured that the induced currents still found a way inside to the electronics all connected and integrated into each module. Their handheld electronics and--more importantly--their suits, unconnected to the modules' structure, were protected and still worked, but would only sustain each person for a couple of hours. They were kicking the can down death's road of inevitability.

He supposed he should feel lucky, because only ten minutes earlier they had almost lost the whole space station to fire, manually casting off several modules to save the whole. The CMEs' induced electrostatic charges had ignited the fire. These particular modules were older and didn't have very much shielding, as they had been built by the Russians. *Enough said.* R.T. figured the next CME, due any moment, was probably large enough to have the same effect on the remaining, better-shielded modules. He wanted to change his vote now. *Definitely fire.*

It was cold. They were huddled together in Melanie's research module in hopes of creating a little more warmth. They were tired, spent; most wore a thin layer of soot from fighting the fires minutes ago. They silently stared at each other or out the aft porthole of their module, counting the seconds until the next sunrise, which would heat their module up just enough to take the sting out of the cold. Then darkness and with it the bitter cold of space.

The escape modules were not an option because someone would have to stay behind to release each manually. Even then, there was still very little chance of survival because each module's occupants had to manually deploy its chutes at the right time, something normally done automatically by computers at the correct altitude. Then there was the little matter of running out of oxygen before they landed and could escape the modules.

"I think we all know the situation we are in," R.T. broke the silence, speaking as their commander. "Best I can figure, we have only one shot for any of us coming out of this alive. We draw straws for someone to stay behind. The rest of us split up into the two escape modules, and the winner will manually release each one. As you know, each escape module's occupants will have to guess correctly at the exact moment to pull their chute. Guess wrong, and either you'll burn up during re-entry or you'll crash to Earth at 10,000 miles per hour. Further, you'll have to set your suit's O2 on a barely passable setting, and then have enough left to be able to pop your helmets off before passing out and then suffocating. Any of you surviving that long will probably still die of hypercarbia. Any questions?"

Everyone was silent, their highly intelligent and educated brains already having deduced the same scenario long before their commander spoke.

R.T. held out eight strips of paper, the bottoms covered by the palm of his hand, waiting for someone to begin the lottery of death.

Melanie reached first. "I guess I'll get us started." She drew a long strip of paper, but held back any outward sign of her happiness. No one but R.T., who watched her response, could see it. R.T.'s resolve was strengthened, knowing she would have a chance.

Each participant's strip of paper drawn appeared long. Their reactions were similar but not as reserved as Melanie's: a long release of air upon realization, and then a breath of oxygen and momentary relief sucked into their lungs. When the last participant waited an extended measure of time to choose from what was believed to be a fifty percent chance at death or a remote possibility of life, he too breathed a long sigh of relief. Then, all looked at their commander, all but one of their knowing faces full of acceptance and relief it wasn't them. Tears filled Melanie's eyes.

R.T. held onto the last long strip of paper. To complete his shell game, he stealthily folded the bottom portion of his strip of paper in half with his other hand and presented the now shortened 'straw' to the group quickly, then he thrust it into his suit pocket. "It's on me then. Let's head to the modules," he said, voice devoid of emotion.

32.
The Kill Order
4:05 A.M.
Rocky Point, Mexico

"*Si, padre*," Rodrigo said very animatedly over his cell phone. "I will do as you say. *Gracias, padre.*" He lowered the phone from his ear and ended the call. His father, Felix "El Chorro" Menendez, had just given him the "*orden a matar*," the kill order. He had killed before, to be sure, but never by a kill order. The Death Squad always handled these, but after Ortega Inzunza was taken out by the Mexican government's gunships on the beach a few months ago, he knew his day would soon come. He couldn't have imagined a better target than Max Thompson.

Ever since the day he saved Miguel, Max Thompson had been a thorn in Rodrigo's side. If it weren't for Max's own stupidity, Rodrigo may have never gotten the chance. Hard to believe he would sell guns to the Ochoas. He dug his own hole, and he would be buried in it soon.

He imagined the moment he would point his nickel-plated .45 Colt Commander at Max's face and then pull the trigger. He was relishing this moment, when he realized three faces were staring intently at him.

"*Puto*, stop staring at me," Rodrigo yelled at all three at once. "What are you, a bunch of dogs? Get everyone. We have our order to kill Señor Max and take his guns and drugs. We meet outside in *cinquenta minutos.*"

With orders given, one of the three henchmen, tasked with additional orders, ran outside the office to another room and announced in Spanish to the other men to get their weapons and meet outside in fifty minutes. The other two called the remaining assassins not at the compound, demanding their immediate return.

Ernesto "El Papá" Fernandez, so named because he was the father of 18 children, was also the oldest of Rodrigo's henchmen. More importantly at this moment, he had become a friend of Maxwell Thompson long before Rodrigo's feud with Max started. He knew the reason for Rodrigo's hatred for the man, and so he kept his friendship with Max a secret. Rodrigo also didn't know that their last load of guns actually came from Max. Again, no need to tell Rodrigo. Ernesto was a loyal lieutenant to Rodrigo, but a kill order for Max? He couldn't stand by without helping his friend. While standing by the Tahoe waiting for the rest of his team, he discreetly pulled out his phone and texted Max, warning him of what was coming his way.

"¿Donde estan Julio y Paco?" one of the *asinos* asked from the vehicle behind *El Papá*.

"*El Jefe* already sent them out yesterday to watch Señor Max and to make sure he didn't run when we go there," Ernesto answered in Spanish.

He hoped that he would reach his friend in time.

Less than fifty minutes after the order was given, Rodrigo walked out to find thirteen of his fifteen men in five vehicles idling and ready to pull out.

"Let's kill ourselves a *gringo*," he yelled jubilantly as he climbed into the second vehicle, a shiny black Cadillac Esplanade SUV. His men cheered back at their leader as the caravan of killers drove out of the compound.

THE EVENT

33.

Over Middle Illinois

Nothing went right with John and Steve Parkington's flight. In addition to the amazing but unnerving aurora displays, all their equipment was barely functional. Their radio returned mostly static. The Garmin GPS with XM Weather was inoperable, displaying a fluttering green-red screen. Even the old VOR system didn't really work. Only one piece of navigational equipment was functional: an old compass, providing the only bearing they felt comfortable following. They were, however, blessed with minimal air traffic due to the early hour and the problems grounding most planes. For the last two hours, the airport closures and diversions had caused their greatest concerns. All were from the same problems they were experiencing--the geomagnetic storms that had laid waste to the satellites on which their equipment depended. After being turned away from Denver Airport because of communications issues, they returned east to attempt landing at a regional outside of Lawrence, Kansas. There, they were planning to refill and get more intel on the problems plaguing all pilots. But they were diverted from there as well. Finally, they hoped to make it to the private airport outside of Kansas City, since MCI was closed, but were once again diverted.

Now, fuel was their chief problem. Even with the extended tanks John had installed, they were on fumes.

While John and Steve discussed their very limited options, someplace over a rural area west of Ottawa, Illinois, their engine stopped along with their radio and all other instruments. All the lights in the cockpit flashed once and then went out. It was as if someone had just unplugged an invisible power cord.

The cockpit of even a pressurized Cessna is loud, so much so that the pilot and co-pilot wear headphones both to hear the radio and to speak to each other via intercom. The sudden absence of engine noise was deafening. Almost in unison, they tugged at one side of their headsets, exposing an ear to confirm what their now frozen propeller and all their other impulses screamed. They were in trouble. A whistling sound from the rushing air displaced by the plane's fuselage and a forward sensation being communicated by their inner ears were the only stimuli telling their senses they were still moving. Otherwise, because the dark of early morning, only slightly illuminated by the green spectral display above, it appeared that they had stopped dead in the air.

"We are dead stick," John announced.

Steve heard his dad's muffled voice, unable to see much of his face beside him. The blackness inside the cockpit was thick and unnerving. He ripped off his headphones.

"--confirm. Son, please confirm that you have no readings on your side?" John yelled louder.

"Dad, I have nothing. You too?"

"Affirmative. I have no electronics, but I have full controls."

"How can we not have even lights? Could our batteries die at the same time as the engine?"

"We have bigger issues. We should be close to a small regional around here..." They struggled to see through the blanket of darkness that covered them, looking for lights, any lights. But they were in a rural and somewhat rugged part of Illinois. It seemed the lights were off below as well.

They glided past a light pole and heard a *whoosh-whoosh* sound, just barely missing some structure… a *windmill?* There, in the distance, was a clearing and a cluster of lights.

"There." John pointed to the patch of lights assembled on the ground, a small town of probably a few hundred, and the faintly lit long line of a rural highway leading to it. Steve craned forward to see it

"That's a highway, not an airport," he said, hoping he was looking at the wrong lights.

"Flying beggars can't be choosy. That will have to do." John pushed his hands forward and turned the plane's wheel counterclockwise, while his feet pushed the pedals to counter. The ailerons, flaps, and rudder worked in harmony to bank the plane left and put it on a downward slope.

They could both feel their air speed dropping a couple of knots every few seconds. Steve pushed the wheel forward more to keep their speed up at the expense of a quicker rate of descent.

The new quiet and somber darkness around them lulled their senses into a false calmness that belied the real danger that waited below. The Earth was going to come at them fast. They passed a single light of a large house in the hills, but aside from that and the town lights, it was dark below them. The town's fast approaching lights beckoned them from just below the cowling, growing in strength with each passing second, as their distance closed.

Then the town's lights went out. It was as if the blanket of darkness that followed them in the air was thrown over the town as well, covering all the lights below.

Now panicked, John and Steve swung their heads wildly, searching for anything, glad they could not see the fear in each other's faces.

"How will we see the street now?" Steve felt stupid for asking a question he already knew the answer to.

"At this point, I'll be happy to see anything," John answered.

Breathing slowly, Steve tried to think like a pilot, considering what he would want to know, based on the forty or so hours he'd flown. "What do you think our altitude is right now?" he finally asked.

"Around 1000," John guessed, "maybe less." He popped open his window and the scary peace was broken by the cool 120-knot air rushing into their cockpit.

Steve understood without asking. John was flying by his senses now, and he needed to hear as well as see anything he could to keep from going in nose first or crashing into a structure or trees on the ground.

Their vision appeared to be adjusting to the darkness. *It was the auroras.* They came to the same realization at once. The ground was bathed in a bright green light, enough now that they could see the trees and the fast-approaching ground.

"I see a road," John announced triumphantly. He banked the plane slightly, but then reality sank in; with only two hundred feet of altitude, they were too far away to make it.

"Steve, prepare for a crash landing. At the last moment, you need to tuck forward. You got that?"

John leveled the plane and searched for the cleanest line and a solid tree or structure to take some of their inertial energy away. He was thankful that he'd attended the workshop on crash landing at Oshkosh last year. At least, with little fuel in their tanks, they wouldn't burn.

"I hear you, Dad. I'm not scared."

There. He found his flight line between two tall oaks. Every second a loud *whoosh* sound, announced a passing tree. *Any second now.*

"I love you, son."

"Love you, too," Steve's voice rose in pitch as he unconsciously braced for the impact the moment it happened.

~~~

Over Texas

The intercom and then the pilot's voice broke through the loud hum of the plane's engines, which were working hard, still pushing to keep them upward. "This is your captain speaking. I'm sure you have already noticed the rare occurrence outside your windows. For the same reasons we left O'Hare so late, if you look out now, you will probably never see an aurora display this far south in your lifetimes." Most of the passengers craned and contorted themselves to see the green ribbons of light spread out all over the horizon, so close they felt they could reach up and touch these heavenly objects.

"Soooo beautiful," Stacy exclaimed, momentarily forgetting her fear, which had been constant throughout their flight.

The captain continued, "Because of recent solar activity, we have the pleasure of--"

The lights flickered and the intercom crackled, cutting off the captain mid-sentence. Every head that had been craning to see the beautiful light show turned to regard the cockpit door, hoping their gaze would somehow pierce the door and yield some sort of confirmation that the plane's captain was not as concerned as they were. The engines started to stumble as did the plane's lights, as if some unknown force was sucking up the plane's energy. Little did the passengers know it was just the opposite.

All at once, the engines stopped and the lights were extinguished. The passengers were bathed in silence and an eerie green darkness. They held their collective breath, as if the plane would now float, using the combined air in their lungs.

Stacy's eyes, slightly illuminated by the green glow of the aurora, were filled with terror. Her right hand reflexively reached, grabbed, and squeezed a vise-grip hold on a hand in the seat next to hers. The silence and the shock of the last few seconds were broken by a sheer wave of panic that washed over everyone from the front to the back of the plane like a tsunami. "Oh, my God!" and "The engines!" screamed out of the cabin's green haze.

"It will be all right," Stacy's friend said, calmly squeezing her hand and that of the boy sitting next to her.

Someone yelled something unintelligible, followed by another, and then another, now screeching the same declaration. "FIRE!"

Stacy looked to her left and saw through two of the window seats that the engines on their side were indeed on fire.

Then, everyone could feel it. Their inertia had given way to the greater force pulling on them: gravity. They started to descend, first a little, then a lot. Within a few seconds, they were spiraling out of control, the plane's electronic controls unyielding to the pilot and co-pilot's physical exertion to keep the plane airborne.

Stacy squeezed her friend's hand so hard it was turning blue. She closed her eyes and starting praying the only prayer that came to mind,

"Now I lay me down to sleep
I pray my Lord my soul to keep
And If I die before I wake,
I pray the Lord my soul to take."

34.
Hell Breaks Loose
5:20 A.M.
Rocky Point, Mexico

Most sunrises on their beach were similarly stunning, with almost imperceptible differences in the new day's light, breezes, or the ocean waves. This dawn was different, a foretelling already seen by many, but soon by everyone else. The sky sported an extra deep hue of magenta, more common during cloudy mornings, and an unnatural shade of lime. There were no clouds, only the slight wispy red and green ropes: leftovers from the evening auroras. These heavenly, ethereal cords slowly dissipated as the sun stood its ground, as if to command them away, at least for now.

With that, a new day started. It was to be a day no one on Earth would forget.

Max had been up for hours--troubled first by his dreams, vivid visions of death and destruction, then last night's light show, both events seemingly predicting what was coming. From what he understood, the CMEs that hit last night were pretty big, but not big enough to cause the destruction he had been most worried about, including wiping out their technology. Unfortunately, that was the mission of their much bigger brothers, traveling on their heels. They were due to hit the Earth at any moment. Unlike solar flares, which carry excessive radiation, coronal mass ejections were large clouds of plasma that weren't directly injurious to humans, but were deadly to just about everything electronic. This one was supposed to be a doozy, potentially many times worse than the Carrington Event of 1859 had been.

Because he'd prepared for this for years, and last night had given Bill and Lisa their instructions, there was little he could do but wait.

His lack of patience for the end of the world to hurry up and get here tickled his desire to find out how much damage the already-arrived CMEs caused elsewhere. While the world still had power, he wanted to watch some news. He turned his TV on, which like his computer equipment was connected to a set of twenty-five backup batteries, charged by the multiple solar roof panels and shielded along with his office behind the bookshelf. However, because both television and Internet were receiving their signals from satellite, Max doubted the reception would be good due to the electromagnetic waves from CMEs. His doubts were correct. It showed nothing but static.

Okay, what next? He rolled over to another table farther back in the warehouse, blew the dust off an SSB receiver, and fired it up. Rotating the Kenwood's dials clockwise, his forefinger and thumb eloquently seeking out any human voice, he could find almost no commercial or ham radio stations. He expected this, since geomagnetic storms also disrupted radio signals. The only somewhat discernible station was a French news broadcast. He was somewhat sure the alluring female voice said that Paris was burning, but his French was rusty and the signal was worse.

He searched his shelves for something, anything that was connected to the world. "Cell phone," he yelped, remembering that he could connect via a Telecell data plan on his phone, which he never used because the cost seemed too expensive. It wasn't a sense of frugality, but a sense of fairness that prevented him from using his data plan. He did not want to support a company that milked the poor people of Mexico. The end of the world was a worthy exception. He stood up from his desk and reached for his smartphone, noticing then that the phone's light was on as if a call, email, or text had recently come through. It was on the shelf above his desk so he hadn't noticed it until now and he forgot he still had the mute switch on since El Gordo's call a few hours ago. More importantly, it occurred to him, he hadn't checked it since he left the WiFi signal from his ranch. He examined the screen and saw five messages:

> Email (25h ago): Cicada Protocol – Open immediately
> Email (24.5h ago): CMERI Bulletin – A Carrington Event is Coming!
> Breaking News (8h ago): Power out in New York – Fires reported
> Worldwide Alert – Killer solar storm coming (16m ago)
> Text (10m ago): Max my friend we are coming to kill you and your f...

He already had read the first message on his computer, which heroically had given its own life to the Cicada cause. He wanted to read the second, third, and fourth items, but then saw the last message's urgency and clicked on it. The text read:

Max my friend we coming to kill you and your friends. We leaving in few minutes. They know you selling guns to Ochoa. Run! God be with you. Pappa.

Ten minutes ago? He grabbed a .45 Glock from the weapons resting atop his workbench and slipped the scabbard gloved to the already loaded pistol over the back of his pants, under his shirt, where the coolness of the weapon against his back provided comfort. Grabbing an extra magazine and running down the hallway while shoving it into his back pocket, he slid in his stocking feet. *Shit. No time to grab my boots.* Punching the door release with his palm, he shoved it open, pivoted and then just as quickly closed it, stopping for just a moment, thinking of one last thing he might have to do. He grabbed an empty journal from his bookshelf and walked over carefully to his little Mexican work desk, across from the bookcase, situated so he could do work and see the ocean. Quickly, he scribbled something on the first page, closed it and placed it on top of a shelf just below the desk surface, making sure it was obvious to anyone who looked for it. Finally, he dashed over the threshold of his patio, to reconnoiter hurriedly with Bill, Lisa, and Sally before Rodrigo's men arrived. He hit a wall of realization, momentarily stopping to assess and let his mind catch up with his eyes. There were two major problems besides their being on a drug kingpin's hit list.

First, his backyard, patio, and pool area were a mess. Scattered among the debris of what had been his tidy patio were the carcasses of many various ocean birds. A pelican's giant body lay face down, with one colossal bloody wing sticking straight up and through what used to be the glass top of a metal patio table. Blood, glass, and other organic matter pooled below its frame, a memorial to an event that puzzled him. At least a dozen other dead birds lay scattered all over the patio, and another dozen or so in the pool, which had a rosy hue to it. The body of a seagull floated, its dying twitches causing slight undulations in the pool's water.

The second problem was that his house and patio lights were out. All should have been on right now even though it was daytime. He flipped a switch confirming there was no power, except of course in his office, which was on a different circuit.

These puzzles were for later.

He leapt into a run, mentally taking an S-shaped route around the debris. His footfalls, muffled by their wet sock coverings, made *plat-ploof, plat-ploof* sounds as he negotiated the obstacles, slipping slightly on each turn. Passing two stacked chairs overturned in a muddle of reddish water dripping into the pool, he heard buzzing, followed by something sharp biting his wet mop-like feet and right arm, like several pinpricks at once. He bounded past the assault, rubbing his arm, uninterrupted, leaving wet footprints on the few dry areas of his pool decking.

A noise from the ocean drew his attention. A scream as a kayaker held her paddle up with erect arms, her body convulsing, and her hair rigidly crowning a face locked in pain. Then it hit him: *electrical current.*

"Lisa, move away from the electrical box!" he screamed over their walls. Lisa turned toward him, her finger poised a foot from their outdoor breaker panel. A snakelike arch of current, inches away, crackled ready to strike at its soon-to-be newly found ground source.

"Get the fuck back," Max yelled this time. Lisa obliged, looking at their bushy-haired friend as he cleared the coffee gate in one stride--a gold medalist making record time--running and shouting at her.

A glint of light serenaded her eyes over Max's head. A growing whistle noise like that of a train announced the arrival, coming quickly. Its silver coat reflected the sun and the greenish sparkling clouds, fragments of yesterday's eve. It was a plane with a tail of black cords, trailing the corkscrewing fuselage. The whistle sound and fuselage heralded what was now unmistakable.

"The plane is going to crash!" Lisa announced her realization, adding a physical exclamation mark with her extended right finger and arm, which followed the doomed aircraft's trajectory until they both met the horizon. Her arm and finger were defeated, unable to save the plane. A bright red-orange mushroom cloud rose in the distance.

Max, now at her wing, and Lisa both fell momentarily silent.

Then the words poured out. "Oh God. That hit the port. That could be Darla and Danny. We need..."

Max grabbed her roughly and ushered her to the patio door. "Hey. That hur..."

"Where are Bill and Sally?" he brusquely interrupted. Crossing the threshold, he demanded, "Where?"

"Did you flip the switch?" Bill was walking towards them from the kitchen, providing half the answer.

"Where's Sally?" Max ignored Bill's question.

"I think..." Noticing his wife's tears, Bill frowned. "What's wrong, honey?"

Shaking like a leaf fluttering on a tree in the wind, Lisa was consumed by grief. "They're all dead."

"Who's dead?" Bill asked, unsure what she was talking about.

Frustrated, Max yelled, "Where the fuck is Sally?"

Bill went silent, and Lisa was still sobbing, arms crossed around her chest. Both looked at their friend.

"I'm here, Uncle Max. It just happened, didn't it? We just got hit by a Carrington Flare again, didn't we?" Sally saw her mother's anguish and rushed over to her, Bill already at her side. "Mom, what's wrong?"

Max tried to get their attention back. "It doesn't matter now, just listen..."

"Oh God, Dar and Danny, everyone on that plane, the kayaker, they're all dead," Lisa shrieked hysterically, sobbing now in Bill and Sally's arms.

"Lisa, that wasn't Dar and Danny. It was some other plane," Max stated emphatically.

"How do you know?" Bill asked the question now on all their minds.

"It was coming from the wrong direction, and I don't think their plane even made it up in the air."

Another explosion interrupted. This one was much closer.

Bill, Lisa, and Sally stopped listening, craning their heads around the limits of the back windows, attempting to find a visual answer to the illogical clues assaulting their senses.

"Please, I need your attention," Max shouted.

~~~

Monroe, Michigan

Uta Parkington was running faster than in any race she had ever run. When she did run marathons, it was with a clear head and lots of time to think. Now she was running for one reason, fear. She figured she had a minute, maybe less, before the Monroe power plant blew up.

Only ten minutes ago, everything at the board had gone crazy. That was when the first anomaly occurred, a spike in the current readings in the Number One. Then, there was a spike in the Number Two. Finally, the whole board had gone red. She had never before seen this happen.

When the Number One caught fire, she was perplexed, having no idea how this could even occur. The coal used to fuel each of the burners is separated until it is needed to limit fire damage potential. So, other than what was fueling the burner and a small supply outside of it, there was nothing to combust.

Then Numbers Four and Five started spiking at the same time. It was then that she knew they were in big trouble because their output hit 125% of capacity: a figure that was impossible to explain. They were only supposed to generate a maximum of 3,300 megawatts, but somehow, they were now over 4,000.

Then she remembered the bulletin a staff member had printed and brought in from the CME Research Institute. It predicted a Coronal Mass Ejection, which would induce current, causing over-capacity in power plants, even those properly shielded from EMPs. *They were not properly shielded.*

"Punch up camera one-six for me, Val," she asked a bald man sitting at a keyboard in front of a couple dozen monitors mounted on the south wall of their control center. An image flickered for a minute, and then the cam from the parking lot showed its image in full color. They could see the secondary parking lot and Lake Erie in the background. It looked like the sky was on fire.

Most of the control room staff stopped their frantic scurrying around the control room, and each tried to make sense of what they were seeing.

Val put the feed up on the main panel screen, twenty feet by twenty feet of vivid color.

In the distance, the transmission lines appeared to be a rope of fire, coming toward their screen. It was like some sort of gargantuan fuse, and they were the explosive.

"Val, hit the alarm and make the announcement. We need to get out of here, now."

That had been maybe two minutes ago.

Uta rounded the last corner, followed by a dozen of her staff, mostly from the control room. An alarm blared in the background and a red light flashed above their heads every 20 feet. There was only 50 feet to go before they would be able to exit and clear the facility.

We might actually make it, she started to hope to herself.

With more violence than what was generated from the sum of all bombs dropped on Dresden, Germany at the end of World War II, the entire Monroe power plant exploded.

~~~

Clear Lake, Michigan

Fred was worried about his granddaughter and grandson. Darla was supposed to send an email or text to let him know they made it on their flight; they should have arrived in Tucson by now. He turned on his desktop computer, set up by his eldest granddaughter, Sally, a couple of years ago and waited for it to boot. He always found this to be a funny way to say it's turning on.

He opened his email. Nothing.

He pressed the Home button of his iPhone to turn it on. It was another marvel of technology. He swiped his forefinger across the screen to unlock it, and then he dialed her cell number. "The number you have called is not available at this time," said a stranger's voice, probably from her provider.

There must be something wrong with the network.

Opening a new email to Dar, he started typing when the computer shut down. He raised his hands and arms almost in surrender, instinctively wondering what he'd touched to cause this. The inside lights were out as well, along with the refrigerator compressor, which always made noise. Its silence was noisier to him.

He pressed the Home button on his iPhone again. It was dead, too.

The smell of smoke reached his nose. Standing up, he walked slowly towards the back patio and saw the wood roof of his metal shed was on fire, as was his neighbor's house.

"Freddie, the house is on fire," yelled his panicked wife from upstairs as he ran outside.

35.
Death is Coming
Rocky Point, Mexico

His driver opened the hood, feeling a sharp pain on his fingertips. Letting go quickly, it closed, the latch engaging again. Rodrigo and two of his men stared at him and the car.

"What is the problem, *puto*" Rodrigo yelled at the driver, who was sure the engine to the Cadillac was not the only thing that was dead.

"I don't know, Rodrigo. All the engines are dead, and I just got shocked. It doesn't make sense," the driver replied, sweating profusely even though it was early morning.

After turning from Fremont onto Camino Playa Encanto, a dirt road two and a half miles from the beach and his target, all their trucks died at the same time. It had to be some sort of trick. Maybe Thompson was onto their plan. Maybe somebody had tipped him off.

"That *puto* Max Thompson is not going to stop us with his tricks. Grab your guns. We walk the rest of the way."

~~~

"Again, I don't think Darla and Danny are on any planes. I think they haven't taken off"--it was more of a hope but he wasn't about to tell them this—"and at this moment, we don't have time to discuss it." Max pleaded with Bill, Lisa, and Sally in the Kings' living area. Lisa had finally settled down a little bit, her body still shaking.

Keeping his voice as calm as he could manage, Max

167

continued. "You'll remember I told you last night that I was pretty sure that we would be hit by a coronal mass ejection from the sun. Well, we are experiencing that right now. All power is out everywhere, and none of your electronics will work. And, you must watch out not to get electrocuted, which is possible around large sources of metal and water. We will survive this because I have about two years' worth of supplies for all of us. But you have to listen to me carefully."

Lisa already had looked at her watch and then held it to her ear, just to make sure it wasn't working. It was a gift from Bill a couple of years ago, a combo digital and analog watch. The digital display was definitely not working. Sally examined her iPhone and after pushing the side and top buttons, she looked up at Max. Bill was banging on the emergency strobe/radio/flashlight contraption he'd bought from an airline magazine last year, hoping that repeated beatings would prove Max's words wrong.

"I know, they don't work," Max emoted, making plain his frustration. "I'm sorry to say this, but they may never work again. The world you knew is over. From this point forward, we all need to concentrate on one thing and one thing only: survival." Max looked at each of the Kings again to make sure his friends were paying attention to how serious he was at that moment.

"We have the supplies that everyone will run out of in a few days. In a few weeks, they will try to kill you for them. In a month, they will be killing each other. Then it will get really bad. Do you understand what I am telling you?"

"Max, how do you know what's happening? How do you know it's this bad?" Sally asked, seeming to keep her wits about her better than her parents were.

"I will tell you all of this later. Bill, you already know some of this." Lisa's and Sally's heads both spun around to Bill with questioning glances, wondering what Max meant. "But we don't have time to talk about this right now. Under no circumstances should you ever tell anyone about what you have here or what I have. You must lie. Your lives and mine depend upon it. Do you understand me?" Max sternly looked at each of them.

The Kings just stared at Max as if as if they were monkeys at a zoo hearing Shakespeare being read to them... They were in shock.

"Do you understand me?" Max screamed at them.

"Yes," they collectively answered.

"Good. Now, Lisa and Sally lock up the house tight and meet me out back in five minutes. Do not do anything else but that." Max looked at both of them to make sure they acknowledged and accepted their task.

"Bill, I need your help across the street." Max, Bill, and Lisa walked briskly to the front door, while Sally headed to the bedrooms to make sure the windows and doors were secured.

When they were through the door, Max turned and said more quietly to Lisa, "Make sure all your windows are secured too, and the blinds drawn. Lock this door behind us. Again, wait out back for me. I have a job for Bill." Max didn't wait for acknowledgement before turning toward the street. Bill and Max jogged to the beach warehouse. Max was still in his damp stocking feet.

36.

Fighting for Your Family

"What the hell is this, another damned surprise?" Bill growled when they crossed into the threshold of Max's beach warehouse. Bill had just realized when he saw the two-story tank that occupied most of the inside of the house that the house was a fake.

"Holy crap, Max, you *really* knew this was coming, didn't you?" He realized his question was mostly rhetorical.

"There's no time. Come here," Max commanded from the spiral staircase in what would have been the dining room. Max went up first, Bill right on his heels. At the second floor, Max grabbed some binoculars and a pair of Tevas he quickly swapped with his socks, and then made his way to the outside terrace above. Bill followed a few seconds behind, trying to come to terms with what was happening around him. Each floor was a new level of reality mugging him. He did not want to know what was on the roof.

Bill mounted the terrace, questions about to break from his lips, but the smoke and fire outside separated him from reason. "Oh, my God... isn't that the Andersons' place *on fire?*" Bill pointed to a beachside house four lots away from where they stood. It was ablaze, and it wasn't the only one. There were fires everywhere in Rocky Point. A chorus of screaming, yelling, and crying mixed with a black haze of smoke that hung over the entire city, and over them was a nightmarish vision he never would have imagined possible in a place that had brought so much happiness to him and his family over the years.

"Good, I don't see them." Max ignored Bill's distress. "We may have a little time still. Their car probably died like everyone else's," he stated in a disconnected matter-of-fact tone, his back turned to Bill and the apocalyptic scene surrounding them, searching for their adversaries with the binoculars.

"Bill, let me have your attention." Max spoke calmly, but sternly. Bill turned to find him seated on a shelf that ran around the circumference of the terrace. Beside him was the sniper rifle cannon Max had showed him only two days ago. It appeared to be set up, pointing inland, as if he intended to use it on someone. Bill quickly stole a glance in that direction, past Max, hoping not to see someone, or what it might mean if they did.

"Bill?" Max waited until Bill was focused only on him. "I am sorry to do this to you. I promise I will explain everything to you fully, but we just don't have time right now. Here is what you need to know. First, as I told you, we have been hit by several large bursts of plasma from the sun yesterday and this morning. We saw this with the green and red auroras. Their induced currents spark fires, like with the Andersons', in anything with enough conductive material. The Smiths' house should be next. Much worse, those currents have destroyed, or are currently destroying, everything that has an integrated circuit, such as a computer, a smartphone, your TV. That's why I had you put everything into your protected room. All cars, except those made before the 80's like Stanley or my Jeep, will no longer run. All power and water are down. All communications including radio and TV are out. And it is *very* important you understand this. This," Max held his arms up, extending them forward and back, "is happening everywhere. It is worldwide. There is *no one* coming to help us, *ever*."

In spite of the many previous warnings, and what Max had shown him, and his wife's losing it earlier, the enormity of what was happening to all of them hit Bill at that moment.

"Max," his eyes tear-filled as he pleaded with his friend, "what about Darla and Danny? How can you be sure they're not flying right now, or that they're safe?"

"In reality, I can't, Bill. I'm sorry, I know this is a gigantic worry for you, Lisa, and Sally. But there is absolutely nothing you can do about it right now. We do know this: if they aren't on a plane, they're smart kids. They'll be safe. However, Bill, at this moment, I need you to concentrate, okay?" Max stopped and waited until Bill nodded in the affirmative.

"We will deal together with surviving this new world, but you must listen to me now." He paused, collected his thoughts, and continued. "There are anywhere from five to twenty men headed this way to kill us. Do you understand what I'm telling you?"

"What? Who? What the hell are you talking about?" Bill's words nearly tumbled over one another.

"The local Mexican cartel knows about my supplies and, unfortunately, about my helping broker an arms deal with another cartel in Northern Mexico near my ranch. Before you say anything, I did what I had to do to get this place stocked up so that we can protect ourselves. But, unfortunately, the son of the local cartel kingpin wants me dead and your family too, and they're coming now to try to kill us."

"Well then, let's get into our truck and leave," Bill interrupted. "You said our cars will run, so let's leave. Why in God's name do you want to play war with people who enjoy killing?"

"Bill, you don't understand. Where would we go? Sally's house in Tucson? How much food does she have? How much water? When that's gone, then what? The world as you knew it is over. Welcome to the Stone Age, my friend. I have two years' worth of food, water, and other supplies, for all of us. Plus, we have a defensible position here. We need to sit tight and not run away from this.

Additionally, I need *you* to take a position up here, and if they show, you need to shoot them. You probably won't need to shoot more than just the leader. The rest of the group will run away when he's dead. They hate and fear him, which is why they will run."

"What? Are you fucking crazy? No way. I am *not* shooting someone." Bill was as angry as Max had expected.

"I'm sorry, Bill, but your life and the lives of your wife and daughter depend on this."

"Why the hell don't *you* stay up here and shoot these people yourself? They're after you anyway."

"I need to go secure your wife and daughter in my safe room. I promise I won't be too long and if they don't show before I return, it's probably not a problem. If they do, you really need to do this. I know you can shoot. We've hunted together, and you're a better shot than me, by far. If they do show up, just remember, they are coming here to *kill all of us*."

Feeling somewhat deflated, Bill asked, "How the hell do you know all of this? How do you know they're even coming?" He felt flushed, with perspiration now soaking his shirt, and daunted by the inevitability of the grotesque task Max was laying out for him. He gave up his resistance, knowing Max well enough that he would not ask unless it was absolutely necessary.

"I got a text, before the power went out. A longtime friend of mine is part of this cartel. He told me about twenty minutes ago that they were headed here. If there wasn't this little problem with the world ending, they would already *be* here. I hope that they won't come, but the little prick leading them will probably walk on foot to get here, which means it could be another ten minutes to two hours."

Max seemed to hesitate, looking past Bill for just a moment before continuing, speaking with surety. "I need to go and make sure your wife and daughter are safe. I will be back in maybe fifteen to twenty minutes, which I figure is what it will take to secure them in my secret office and tell them what they need to know. You know they'll be safe there. We can all talk in detail then.

"One more thing. I see you have your key. It works on this place as well. If anything happens to me, or if you don't hear from me in, say, one hour, come down, lock up, and go to the safe room. Make sure no one sees you." Max was already halfway down the staircase by the time he finished.

"Max, please take care of my family," Bill begged, finally accepting what would be the most difficult job he had ever undertaken.

"With my life, I promise." Max gave a reassuring glance and was gone.

~~~

After securing the front door, Max crossed the street, carefully checking to see if there were any threats, his hand instinctively finding the form of the gun hidden underneath his shirt. No one was outside. He continued through his beach house's front gate, walking carefully and precisely, around the front and down the side yard that separated his and the Kings' property. He quietly drew his .45 and held it toward the ground, at the ready. Just before he had given Bill a bitch-slap to reality, he watched two armed men come from the beach side and ascend the stairs of both his and the Kings' house and then to the patio doors. At first he didn't think they were Rodrigo's men, because Rodrigo preferred a more garish display of force, with guns blazing. Rodrigo's perversion was the theatre of killing, with AK-47s acting as protagonists. However, if they *were* Rodrigo's men, he reasoned that they would want to capture him, Bill, and his family alive, so that Rodrigo could start the show when he and his other men arrived. Max was sure Rodrigo hadn't arrived yet, because his goons would have made their presence known, using fear to their advantage. Therefore, these two were most likely either waiting to ambush Max from the outside or they had taken Lisa and Sally hostage and were waiting for him inside the Kings'.

Making sure that no one saw, he hopped the property wall and dropped down below their dining room window, keeping tight to the wall.

He rose slowly, lifting his head slightly above the windowsill so that he could see into the Kings' home. There, on the sofa, were a very scared-looking Lisa and Sally with some young thug standing behind them.

A barely perceptible crunch sound came from Max's left shoulder. A man's booted footfall sounded on the rocks, probably the other one of the two he had seen. Max immediately spun around and dropped to the ground, pointing his gun, finger on the trigger. He had a perfect sight picture, training it on the perp's forehead. He wanted this done with one shot.

The man neither heard nor saw him; his AK was slung loosely, hanging on his side away from Max. He was probably investigating another part of the house or looking for Max.

An explosion sounded from another house a few doors

down. The man looked up, first surprised and then puzzled as he caught a glimpse of Max. Clumsily, and in slow motion, the man tried to grab and raise his weapon when Max squeezed his trigger.

~~~

Bill was sweating more than he could remember ever having sweated before. The sun beat down on him unmercifully, the canopy offering no protection to the back part of the terrace, adding to the difficulty of what he had to do. He counted fourteen men walking their way, having shown up moments after Max left. They marched in a V formation like a flock of seagulls, with their leader at the point. That was the man he was supposed to shoot. Bill had the gun sight trained on him.

He felt as if he was on the precipice staring down into hell's fire. He was sure if he squeezed the sniper rifle's trigger, his soul would follow.

"Oh God, am I really going to do this?" Bill mumbled. "Am I really going to squeeze the trigger and send a bullet into this stranger's body, taking his life? Why again am I doing this? Because this man is *maybe* a threat to my family or me? What kind of reasoning is this?" Bill muttered this to the one man he saw through the eyepiece. Each man except the leader appeared to have an AK assault rifle slung in front of his chest or at his side.

An explosion nearby wrenched Bill's attention away from his target. Through the fire and billowing, black smoky haze, he recognized it was the Smiths' house only five doors away, next door to the Andersons'. Max had said it would go next because of the metal in the structure, through which the magnetic waves induce current and overload the circuits, causing it to blow, or some such logic.

He then looked at his house and Max's. *God, please protect my family.*

<center>~~~</center>

Lisa was past the point of panicking. This nervous Mexican man looked like he was going to kill them. So did his partner who had gone back outside several minutes ago. *What did they want?* she wondered. *Why us? And what if either Bill or Max wandered in on them?* She said a quick prayer.

At the *amen,* an explosion rang out a few houses away. Both Lisa and Sally jumped slightly out of their seats. The twitchy Mexican holding them hostage, the younger of the two, scuttled toward the patio door, probably to look outside and see what caused the explosion.

The sharp crack of a gunshot blasted right outside their dining room window.

"Oh God, Daddy!" Sally shrieked. Lisa squeezed her hand even tighter.

The young Mexican, already half out the patio door, turned back inside and ran toward the window and the sound of the gunshot with his rifle slung forward and pointed in front of him. When he was at the window, he was startled to see Señor Max, the man they were after, rise up slowly outside, near the window, pointing his pistol toward the street. He was about to surprise Señor Max. Lifting his rifle level to his right eye, the young Mexican's barrel bounced around with his heavy breathing and fear. But it was hard to miss at this distance, and Señor Max still hadn't turned around. His finger curled around the trigger. He started to apply pressure.

<center>~~~</center>

Max quietly and slowly rose, staying out of the view of the window. He kept his gun steady on the man he'd shot in the head, making sure he wasn't a threat any longer. Satisfied, he turned toward the window to deal with the next bad guy--who was already standing behind the window with his gun pointed directly at him.

The gunshot caused Max to jump and stumble back a couple of steps, as he also futilely attempted to meet the assaulter with his own weapon. However, it was too late. He was in shock, not from being shot but from seeing the young Mexican's chest explode through the window and then his body collapse out and onto the windowsill, where he came to rest, a flop of matted black hair hanging below his head. Max instinctively felt his body for some evidence of the wound he had to have. His mind and body attempted to reconcile and make sense of what just happened. *Maybe it was Sally or Lisa?* His mind wrestled with the only plausible answer.

Satisfied he was unharmed, he briskly walked to the Kings' back patio door. In the doorway, partially obscured by the curtains swaying with the ocean breezes, a man pointed a gun at him.

~~~

Bill heard the gunshot, just below the terrace. Maybe a minute later, he heard another one that resonated below, this time more muffled.

"Dammit. Focus, Bill," he yelled, lowering his face again behind the eyepiece of the .50-caliber Barrett sniper rifle. The sight picture was instantaneous, and his target was drawing closer.

However, the damned image wouldn't stay still. The lead stranger was walking toward him, but the heat distortion of the dusty Mexican road added a surreal quality to the landscape in his eyepiece, as if just below and out of sight the desert was on fire. Bill was shaking. In spite of the firmness of the gun's bipod and the 90-degree heat, he was chilled by the awful task given to him. His chest was pounding so hard, he felt as if his ribs were being bruised from the inside by each rapid beat of his heart. The heat, the humidity, the movement of his enemy, his fear, all conspired to cause his target to dance around in the rifle's crosshairs, which he was having more and more difficulty holding steady over the man's body. *You can do this.*

He enjoyed hunting animals and he had taken down many over the years, albeit with weapons far less complicated and powerful. But he had never shot a person, thankfully. Even with their Christian faith, his wife and he never questioned their stance on killing someone who had broken into their house or threatened their family, having discussed this possibility on numerous occasions. That scenario had always seemed easy. After all, it would be defensive and perhaps reactionary, with no time to think. The contemplation before pulling *this* trigger was certainly different. *But, isn't it also defensive?* he reasoned.

The picture laid out for him by Max was pretty straightforward. *Henchmen for the cartel are approaching from the north by foot. They intend to kill you, your family, and me, but if you shoot the leader, the others may go away and not bother us. If you don't shoot, they will kill us all.*

He knew he had to do this. His wife's, his daughter's, and his friend's lives depended on his doing this. His indecision started to shrink slightly now.

The advanced eyepiece gave him more information than he wanted to know. Strange these electronics even worked, when everything else didn't, from what Max had said. He considered the most important facts it provided: Distance to target: 1857... 1856 meters, Temperature: 90.6, Humidity: 57.4%. He considered how much the bullet would drop, but shrugged it off, knowing that even if it dropped a foot, this missile would stop its intended target.

"But the leader isn't even armed," Bill said out loud, offering a last-minute defense.

He wiped away the discolored beads of sweat dripping down from his dirty brow, about to further blur his vision. The unshaded back area of the terrace allowed the sun to make the gun and his hands and body feel as if they were on fire. The humidity from the sea made it that much more miserable. His dirty t shirt stuck to his back like a second skin.

Just then, he noticed it. The leader also had a sling around his chest.

All his attention now focused on what was connected to the sling. Was it a satchel or something worse? The answer was unmistakable. The short black barrel of an automatic rifle revealed itself from behind the man's back with every other step of his stride. Case closed.

The image was now still, as was his resolve.

He squeezed the trigger. The blast was deafening.

~~~

"Come in, Señor Max," said an icy calm voice with a thick Mexican accent that spoke violence.

Max walked through the entry and curtains and saw Lisa and Sally huddled together on the couch, valiantly attempting to suppress their terror and tears. Their wide-eyed gazes were trained on Max and the man in front of them, pointing a gun at Max. Max turned to the man and could see his unmistakable short-cropped hair and small scar on his check. It was Chaco, one of El Gordo's men. Not knowing if he should celebrate or fear what was coming next, he asked, "Are you the one I have to thank for saving my life?"

A shot rang out. Max recognized the thunderous report instantly, greeting it with both happiness and sorrow.

With the icy conviction of a killer, not even flinching at the noise behind him, Chaco said with a sneer, "Don't feel too rested, Señor Max. We going to see *El Jefe* now."

"Señor Luis here? He is in Rocky Point?" Max's voice betrayed his worry.

"No, Señor Max, we go to da *rancho de El Jefe*."

The front door opened noisily, and another of El Gordo's men sauntered in with the leisurely gait of a homeowner walking into his own front entrance, the assault rifle slung around his neck breaking this illusion. He quickly said something unintelligible to Chaco in Spanish, who had turned away from Max for just a moment.

Turning back to Max, Chaco said, "We go in your car, because ours no work. Let's go now. *El Jefe* want you talk now," he said pointing to the front door. "And no one else comes. If we see anyone follow, your friends not be happy with result. *Entiendes?*"

Max nodded in agreement and then turned to Lisa and Sally. "Bill is up on my other house roof. Lisa, you'll need to support him, because I made him do something to protect you both. Stay here and wait for him. When you see him, tell him what happened to me and that I don't want any of you to follow. I'll come back, although it might be in a few days. Tell Bill to use the key he has to my office. Tell him to grab the book under my desk. You'll both need to read what's in there." When he saw Lisa's questioning look, he finished. "It's all right, he'll understand. You'll all be fine now, I made sure of it."

Sally leaped up and in a desperate attempt to keep him from going, threw her arms around Max. "Uncle Max, please, you can't leave. We're so scared."

"You'll both be fine. If I don't return in a few days, don't worry, it's probably just my Jeep or what's going on around us."

He released Sally with a kiss on her cheek and kissed Lisa goodbye in kind. He walked to the front door flanked by El Gordo's goons.

"Remember the book," Max offered as he walked out, back into the heat of the day, then looked up to see if he could see his friend.

~~~

Bill looked again through the eyepiece to confirm he had killed the leader and that all his men had run off. One man stood composed, unmoving and staring in his direction, although Bill knew there was no way he could be seen from this direction without the aid of a powerful scope like this one. The men around this one confident fellow were either cowering in fear or had already vanished. One other, the leader he'd shot, lay prone and unmoving in a growing pool of his own blood.

The confident man forced a grin right at Bill, as if saying *I've got your number, buddy.* For the third time today, Bill felt a chill down his sweat-soaked back. Then the man turned his back to Bill, readjusted his gun, and walked away. The cowering men slinked after him.

Bill grabbed the cannon and ran to the front of the terrace, cycling another round into the chamber. He desperately needed to see what had happened to his wife and daughter, and to Max. Just as he looked down, resting the barrel of the cannon on the lip of the wall's edge, two men were walking Max out his front door. He was done shooting people for the day, and didn't want Max's encouragement to save him, not yet holding the weapon up to fire.

Max was already looking up and staring at him. Bill looked at him expectedly, fearful Max wanted him to shoot these two men, and raised a free hand, palm up, asking *what should I do?* Max held his two palms at Bill and shook his head as if to answer *no.* Bill watched him walk to his Jeep, parked outside in front of the garage. They got in, Max in the driver's seat; it started, and they drove away.

Not wanting anything more to do with the rifle, Bill set it on the shelf protected by the wall. He bounded down the stairs and out the door, fumbling with his lanyard and key, trying to lock it as instructed. Now frantic for news about his wife and daughter, he galloped to his house. He felt exposed, as if another dozen or so mass murderers with rifles were going to rush into the street with guns blazing. His paranoia was thankfully just that.

When he was about to cross the front-door threshold, he yelled out their names. "Lisa? Sally? Where are you?" He was half way down the hall when four outstretched arms embraced him, squeezing him very hard. Like a blanket, their embraces and tears covered him with warmth and peace.

Lisa and Sally unleashed a fusillade of colorful descriptions of the preceding minutes. Bill said very little, holding tightly to what he had to do. For their parts, Lisa and Sally never let on that they knew he had done something unsavory, and they never asked. When they got to the part of Max's abduction, surrender, and then Max's final request, Bill jumped in. "Wait, he wanted to go with them?"

"They were quite insistent," Sally answered, "but it looked to me like he knew these people. They certainly knew Uncle Max."

"Do you know what he meant about the book?" Lisa chimed in, having calmed down considerably, her curiosity now getting to her.

"No, I have no idea. Although, he did tell me he planned to give us lots of detail about his plans for us, but he certainly couldn't have known about leaving us. Let's go find out."

Lisa looked past Bill to the dead man hanging out their dining room window. "How do we know they are all gone?" She jerked her head in the dead man's direction. Her question felt surreal to her, as if she were asking how the china looked on the table of their dining room, when there was in fact a dead man resting in their window.

Bill turned, and stepped back, his mind catching up with his eyes. *That explains one of the gunshots.*

"I think there's another outside the window," Sally offered.

And that explains the second gunshot I heard. Bill's mind ran through the events. "Max seemed pretty sure that the others would run aw… that there would be no more, than those two."

~~~

A few minutes later, after more hugs and a little more sharing of today's events, Bill pushed the dead man the rest of the way through their window; the blast had done most of the work for him. Surprisingly, there was almost no blood in the house. All of the gore was on their windowsill and outside.

The three of them, holding hands for comfort and protection, walked out back toward Max's home, gingerly stepping around the dead birds that littered their yard, then around a greater number in Max's yard. None of them questioned this, their senses numb from what they had already witnessed. Bill led, walking them through Max's patio doors and toward the bookcase.

Lisa, bringing up the rear and letting go of their hand-holding chain, stopped and studied the small desk to their right. "Is that the desk Max talked about? Look, here is the book," she said, holding up the volume Max had overtly placed below the desk earlier.

She opened it so that all three could see, not waiting for a reply. It read in hurried script, "Sorry, wrong book."

"No, it must be in his office," Bill said reaching up to the top shelves of the wood bookcase.

"What office?" Sally asked.

37.

Airport Parking

"I have to go pee," Danny said meekly, interrupting Darla's quiet slumber.

She rubbed her eyes and brushed some of her long hair behind her right shoulder, then stretched a little, working out the tightness in her leg from sleeping in one position for such a long time in their car.

"I really have to go," came Danny's voice again, now with more urgency.

"I heard you, kiddo," Darla said as she opened the door to let in the sound of crickets and the heat of the day. "Why don't you go there?" she asked, pointing at an area where the parking lot ended at a fence, protecting some heavily weeded field belonging to O'Hare.

"No, I want a bathroom," Danny protested.

"Sorry, but you know how far the bathrooms are. Unless you want to hold it, you'll have to go there."

"Fine, but don't look," he grumbled as he got out on the opposite side of the car.

She did just that, watching Danny walk to the fence, unzip his pants, and urinate on it, trying his best not to act conspicuous and not hit his shoes. Darla smiled at this and tried not to think about her next decision.

They had missed their flight by almost an hour. When they had arrived at the airport after one in the morning, all the outbound flights had been cancelled, and incoming flights were only accepted because they had nowhere else to go. She'd gotten this information from a pilot, figuring he would be a better source of info than the peons at each flight counter. He'd told her all airports were having communication problems, and they could do little more than wait. Until further notice, all flights were cancelled. There was no place to stay. Every place she called was booked, and then they were having problems making phone calls at all. It seemed like the whole cell network had gone dead.

Without the ability to call, she'd tried texting her father, then Sally, then her grandfather, and finally Steve. It didn't appear that any texts went through. Finally, exhausted from the driving, the late hour, and trying to negotiate a flight, lodging, and everything else, Darla gave up. "We're going back to the car," she announced to Danny. That's when everything had just stopped.

They had just walked past the TSA security lines, which were still long, even though the flights had been stopped for almost an hour. Before they could make it to the exits, all the lights went out. The vast expanse of the airport went black. What was truly odd was the lack of light from anything. There were no headlights from cars right outside and no lights from others' cell phones, either.

At first, most of the crowds were subdued, milling around in sort of a stunned silence, waiting for the lights to come on automatically as they all expected them to. Darla and Danny both stopped their progression out as well, probably more curious than concerned. Then there was a scream, followed by another. Then a rush of footfalls, running, some tumbling. Panic fueled the crowd's motion toward the doors and the eerie, ambient green light outside.

Darla and Danny didn't need much motivation to start moving forward. Someone bumped into Danny, after tripping over the roll-aboard he was dragging behind him, almost knocking him down. Darla held tight and together they ran for the doors, holding hands and dragging their bags. Among the sounds of pandemonium behind them, Darla could hear Danny's labored breathing. He was having an attack.

"We're almost there. Let's get through the doors, and you can use your inhaler."

She directed him around an overturned luggage cart, a dozen or so bags spilled off to the side. Several people were flailing on the ground, having made poor judgment of these obstacles, even though the light from the outside was brighter here.

They were at the door, Darla grabbing Danny's suitcase and yelling over the din of commotion that caught up with them, "Danny, you go first. I'm right behind you." They were ten or so people from the exit, a clogged funnel of people surrounding them, trying to get through their chosen exit. The funnel pressed up against them. *Just five people to go now.*

A loud crashing sound and then an explosion behind them caught everyone's attention and quieted most of those around them. Darla pressed forward, not looking where others were. *Three people to go.*

Danny's breathing was raspy, his lungs trying desperately to get air. An opening was just ahead, as two people fell forward and to the right of them. Darla pushed Danny to the left. *Fresh air*!

Now she steered him to the right about ten feet to an area away from the door. Tossing their suitcases aside, she thrust his inhaler into his mouth, his hands there to guide her. "Breathe slowly, Danny. You're going to be just fine. Take another puff."

His head was a helmet of sweat, his eyes dilated, but he was starting to calm down and his breathing was sounding more normal. He had probably been seconds from passing out. *Whew.*

She took a moment to check out their surroundings outside. Cars were sitting where they had abruptly stopped. People streamed from the exits all around them, like water from a fire hydrant, the flow running in between the cars and any other open spaces. Another explosion to their right, and this time it drew both Darla and Danny's attention. It appeared to have happened around a runway, out of their view, but they both could see the top of the fireball.

"Can you breathe enough to move?" Darla felt like they had to get away from the airport, quickly. She led him again, this time toward where they had parked their car, thankfully a long walk away.

~~~

After they had slept a few hours in the car, her mind felt clearer. She guessed it was mid-morning.

She was now faced with a decision. Their car didn't run, but apparently neither did anything else, for that matter. They had little food and water. Waiting for help wasn't going to work as she was pretty sure there was no help coming for a very long time. No matter where they went, they'd have to go on foot, not an enviable prospect with an asthmatic brother. At this moment, the decision was simple. They would walk the fifty miles between them and their home in Chicago.

She was about to announce her decision to Danny when she smelled smoke, lots of it. Turning toward the airport terminal, she could see its source. Every structure in their path was on fire.

38.

Wright Ranch

Wilber was carrying his MAK-90, a sort of AK-47 knock-off made in China, but tricked out with a synthetic stock and a short tactical scope. He had this gun for years and felt very comfortable with it, having shot maybe ten thousand rounds through it. It was slung around his neck, his hand on the grip, barrel pointed down. He walked quietly, looking for the wreckage of the plane that had crashed on his property a couple of hours ago. He was pretty sure that any survivors were not on his property for nefarious reasons, but you could never be too sure.

His Lab, Trixie, was leading the way, stealthily sniffing and walking through the brush and trees, honing in on something. Of course, the old girl could be hot on the trail of one of the feral cats around here as well.

The creaking noise of grinding metal on metal caught both their attention. It was dead ahead less than a few yards from them.

In a clearing, Wilber could see two of the larger oak trees on his property. He stopped to take in the abnormal picture of two airplane wings, one on each of the side of two large oak trees. A small private plane had flown directly between the two, sheering off its wings. He continued, while Trixie trotted ahead further and out of sight, obviously catching the scent of someone.

Her barking brought him to a run, until he found himself staring at the beat-up rudder of a plane. What was left of the fuselage was wedged into a bramble of bushes and smaller trees. Trixie was on point and growling at the occupants. Wilber couldn't see any movement. With rifle pointed at the cockpit, he carefully walked forward.

Peeking inside, he saw two men. The pilot was bloody and apparently unconscious; the other was moving, having just come to and playing with his open door. Wilber opened the cockpit door, its injured hinges alerting the waking co-pilot to his presence.

"Let me see your hands," Wilber demanded of the co-pilot, who had a small gash on his head, but otherwise looked unharmed. Again he demanded, "Your hands."

The co-pilot lifted his hands up, and pleaded with the gunman. "Please don't hurt us," he begged, glancing to the pilot. "Please help us... my father is hurt."

Wilber re-slung his rifle around his back, assessing they were no threat and needed his help.

"I'm Wilber, this is Trixie, and she won't bite you if you don't make any sudden moves. Are you able to get and come around to help me with your father?"

"Sure, thanks. He's John and I'm Steve."

39.

Crashing to Earth
Out of orbit, over Texas

Melanie's calculating mind found endless folly in her actions, now figuring her chance of survival at maybe one in a thousand. She found much more comfort in her memories, even the sad ones. She thought about her family and friends. She had always been single, married to only her career, and her parents had passed on long ago. So her friends and colleagues were her only family. *What a sad sack*, she thought. Then she thought of R.T. She really had feelings for him. He was attractive and available, being divorced for almost a year now. She laughed at the awkward ways he attempted to hide his interest in her. Yet, he was always professional. That's what first had attracted her to him on this mission. Most men, especially in superior roles, hit on her constantly. It was a maddening affront to all the hours of work she invested in her career.

But R.T. is different... was *different*.

She replayed in her mind the moment she had said goodbye, touching her lips as she did.

Together, they had released the first escape module, sending out four of their comrades. Then, the remaining two and finally Melanie started to enter the second module, when she turned and was nose to nose with him.

"Make it a good life. They'll need you more than ever now," he said just loud enough to be heard. "It was a pleasure knowing you."

She didn't know what possessed her. She leaned forward

and kissed him softly on the lips. "Thank you." It was all that she could muster before he stepped back and closed the hatch, but she could see his face had changed. It was still a face of determination, but also happiness.

The ISS was now a faint dot in space, unremarkable except for the feelings she had left behind.

"Lieutenant?" She registered a distant voice.

Make it a good life.

"Lieutenant?" Conrad's voice from behind pulled her back to reality. "How much buffeting do you think we should endure before pulling the chute?"

It was a good question, and one that she didn't quite know how to answer, even with her advanced degrees. However, she knew it would come to her, at the right moment. She knew it, because she was sure they were going to survive this. *To hell with your mental computations*, she thought. Even if the odds were one in a million, she would bet on the one. She knew they would make it now. A smile formed on her lips. They were the lips she had just shared with another, and they would be shared again.

"Not much longer now."

40.

The Letter
Rocky Point, Mexico

Lisa was agog at all the supplies stacked on the walls. Sally inspected the computer console with admiration. Bill, as directed, reached below Max's desk and found a leather satchel with what felt like a large book inside it. "I think this is it," he announced triumphantly.

Opening the satchel, he reached in and found a wrapped rectangular object, bound together by leather straps, which he placed on top of it. As he pulled on the straps, the hide covering loosened. Bill delicately pinched each corner of the hide, pulling it to the side, revealing its contents. Two white, recently printed pages lay on top of a well-worn, dark leather journal.

He looked up to see Lisa and Sally both anxiously waiting for him to read.

It was a letter with a giant logo, which looked like Max's stylized initials, prominently taking up much of the top of the page. It announced, *From the desk of Maxwell J. Thompson.*

"It's from Max to all three of us." His voice quavered a bit as he read.

To my family (Bill, Lisa & Sally),

It is with deepest regrets that I am not there to deliver this message to you in person. I am writing this to you with a heavy heart, knowing I cannot be there for you. I received a warning from a not-so-nice business partner, Luis Ochoa (he runs the largest drug cartel in Northern Mexico), that another drug gang

STONE AGE

*might go after me. I'm guessing that by your reading this, I am
either dead or have been taken captive.*

*I am hoping I was able to share some of my knowledge
about what is now occurring around us, but in case I wasn't able
to, let me explain this to you now. Our Earth was hit with a
devastating series of coronal mass ejections or CMEs, leading up
to a massive one today. We'll call this The Event, and it
presumably happened after I wrote this. I knew this was coming,
but no one was sure exactly how bad it would be, and most would
have only suspected this to be a one-time occurrence.
Nevertheless, here is a bullet point list of what I believe will
happen worldwide:*

- *All power will be out – All power grids fried. This will
  be permanent and most likely will last the rest of your
  natural lives.*
- *All 20th & 21st technology will be destroyed – from the
  Internet to any solid-state circuit. Anything you turn on,
  and many things you don't, will be neutered. Some will
  explode, melt, or catch fire. So leave all your electronics
  in your safe room as I instructed.*
- *Millions will be electrocuted - Any conductive material,
  while the magnetic waves from a CME are being
  dispersed, may be electrified. This includes the ocean, so
  be wary.*
- *There is not enough food & water available for everyone
  as our system of delivery of all our processed food,
  water, & medicine has been inexorably destroyed.
  Because of this, what follows is most important if you
  want to survive this...*
- *The world around you, including most of the people you
  know, will die. This may sound terribly harsh, but it is*

195

the absolute truth. Deal with it now, so you won't make the wrong choices later.

- *Many people, including those you may call friends, if they do survive, will kill you to get at what I am going to tell you next.*

As you know, I have prepared for this event, but you don't know to what extent. This workshop/office is stocked with guns, ammo, and other non-food supplies. Across the street you'll find my warehouse. It is built to look like a regular house but it actually contains enough food, water, and other supplies for all four of us for the next two-plus years. I have attached to this letter instructions and inventory for accessing all the important areas of this beach house and the warehouse. Bill already has the key to both.

It is worth noting again for your own safety, you CANNOT tell ANYONE about any of this. If you even hint at this, you will be murdered for this information. I'm not just speaking about bad guys. I am saying everyone is your enemy from now on. Within a matter of one to two weeks, the food supply will run out for everyone in Rocky Point. Most will turn to the sea, which--if not electrified--will sustain many, but there will not be enough for everyone, including most of our American friends who don't have the skills to survive in this land. Because of the lack of clean water and no way to wash or to pump sewage, diseases will follow. You must keep everyone away from your home and this home. That means you will (NOT MIGHT) have to shoot even a neighbor to save your life. That is what the guns are for.

The lone exceptions to this are Miguel Fernandez, his wife, Maria, and their soon-to-be-born baby. Miguel has helped me enormously and if he or his wife show up, please take them in.

Miguel has helped me move supplies to this house from my ranch in northern Mexico.

Do not drive your truck or my Jeep around. The Jeep will be one of the few vehicles that work because it uses a points ignition system. The first bad guy that hears you coming will shoot you dead to take your vehicle. This should be held for an emergency only. If the house is overrun, and you can escape, I have provided you with a map so you can go to a place I have secured for you in Colorado. You'll find these instructions in the leather book, including the notes of its original owner, my great-great-grandfather, Russell P. Thompson III.

I don't know exactly what the future holds, but I suspect that the power will not come back on in our lifetimes. That is because I believe the CMEs will continue for years and years, and our magnetosphere that has protected us so far is breaking down, allowing more of the damaging plasma to get through and continue to induce electromagnetic waves throughout our atmosphere. This is what screws up our radio, internet, and solid-state circuitry. Additionally, you'll need to watch out for radiation and UV light from the sun, which will be many times as intense as it is now. I suspect you will see a rapid increase in skin cancer on those who survive the first year. Cover up when you're outside.

I won't lie to you. The life you will now live will be the hardest you have ever experienced. But, you should be able to survive with what I left you. I have faith in you, your abilities, and your love for each other.

I lost my faith when I went to war and had to kill people for my country. The cause was right, but I started to doubt God's existence and doubt whether we are anything more than ants to a creator. Your family has brought me hope and love, and with it, the faith that I lost so many years ago.

I pray that you strive to persevere, even when you will want to give up, that you support one another, and that your love for one another grows. Most of all, survive, for me.

I pray that I will see you again during this life. However, if I don't, I pray that it will be long before we meet again on the other side of death.

God's peace.

Your friend always,

Max

41.

CMERI
Salt Lake City, Utah

The reflection of a solitary figure grew in the polished glass of
CMERI's front door. A man with features wrinkled from a lifetime
of too little sleep, crowned by gray hair and a fedora, sporting a
full grey beard more common to men of a century ago, stopped
arm's length from the handle. Pulling a single page and masking
tape from a leather saddle bag he wore like a backpack, he quickly
taped the sheet to the door and stepped back. He considered his
immediate work and its message. Then he gazed admiringly at his
lifetime of work, represented by this building. He would probably
never see his building again. A lifetime of work was completed.
Now, time to move on to his next two jobs: surviving and getting
to Cicada.

     He turned and walked with purpose to a recumbent delta
trike parked in the middle of the complex's private driveway.
There was no fear of blocking traffic that would never come again.
He mounted the seat and pulled down on the fedora's brim, to keep
the winds from taking it. Pushing forward he began his next
journey, the long pedal of over five hundred miles from Salt Lake
City to Boulder, Colorado. He was thankful the world had ended
during the summer.

     The page taken from his stationery at home usually carried
a Trebuchet font. On this one, he had written by hand in careful

block writing.

From the Desk of Dr. Carrington Reid

THE END HAS ARRIVED. ALTHOUGH I HAVE BEEN PREDICTING THIS DAY WOULD COME, EVEN I WAS UNDERPREPARED FOR ITS ARRIVAL.

WE EXPERIENCED A WORLDWIDE MULTIPLE CME EVENT. OUR SERVERS AND WE BELIEVE EVERY COMPUTER IN THE WORLD, EVEN THOSE WHICH WERE PROTECTED, HAVE BEEN DISABLED OR DESTROYED. ALL ELECTRONICS, INCLUDING ALL SENSORS AND TESTING EQUIPMENT, HAVE BEEN RENDERED INERT.

CMERI'S EXISTENCE SERVES NO FURTHER UTILITY, SO WE HAVE CLOSED INDEFINITELY AND HAVE LEFT TO BE WITH OUR FAMILIES.

MOST SCIENTISTS, LIKE ME, ARE OUT OF A JOB. THE SKILLS WE LEARNED ARE NO LONGER NEEDED IN THIS WORLD. I WISH I KNEW HOW TO FARM OR HUNT. IT MAY BE AT LEAST A GENERATION OR TWO BEFORE WE CAN START USING 21ST CENTURY TECHNOLOGY AGAIN.

I AM GOING TO TRY TO MAKE IT TO COLORADO, TO AN EXISTING COMMUNITY OF HAND-CHOSEN INDIVIDUALS I BELIEVE WILL HAVE THE RESOURCES AND KNOWLEDGE TO REBUILD OUR SOCIETY.

IF ANYONE READS THIS, I'M SORRY I DIDN'T DO MORE TO WARN MORE PEOPLE TO PREPARE. I TRIED.

GOD BE WITH US ALL,

DR. CARRINGTON REID,

FORMER DIRECTOR, CMERI

42.

Powerless
9 Days A.E. (After Event)
Rocky Point, Mexico

The auroras had been gone for a full day now, and it was dark outside--the first total darkness they had experienced since the auroras started. The sky was a carpet of stars and nothing else. The length of the beach, usually lit up like a Christmas tree, was as dark as the night. They could still hear occasional gunfire, but it was otherwise silent.

The Kings were careful not to turn on or use any electronic devices, in case there were any induced currents lurking. Before plugging anything into the house's electrical line, Bill used a current tester to test the line: nothing. Although Max had warned them that their solar panels would be slightly degraded because of the solar storms, he had said they should work, if the storms passed. However, it was dark now, and the panels would provide no help for the next test. Feeling safe, Bill pulled the batteries stored in their safe room and connected them in parallel to the incoming line from the solar panel's control box. Max said they had been fully charged a month ago, so they should still be holding a charge. The other batteries hooked up to the system during the Event were already fried.

They each plugged in a couple of lights around the house. Lisa and Sally stopped in the kitchen, lit by candlelight; they held their collective breath, and both had their arms out and fingers crossed, with expectant expressions. Bill walked to the circuit panel, just outside their patio door. There was nothing more to be said, so Bill flipped the switch.

The lights flickered, and then they turned on.

Like a beacon of an old lighthouse casting its light out to sea, the light from their house cut through the blanket of darkness inside and out, sending beams of brightness everywhere.

All the Kings yelled in excitement, jumping up and down and holding onto each other.

Bill was ecstatic. This was it. Maybe many lives would eventually go back to some sort of normal. Maybe it wasn't going to be as bad as Max had told them.

Air conditioning. Computers. Cold beer.

It might take a long time to restore what was lost, and undoubtedly many would still die, but maybe, just maybe, it would be something like what they had before.

Bill kissed Lisa, knowing she had similar thoughts.

The lights blinked. Then they flickered. Then they went out, this time for good.

The Kings all stopped just as abruptly, frozen in place, afraid to move an inch.

They waited.

Silence and stillness surrounded them. Even the waves barely moved. It was a quiet that seemed unfamiliar.

Two of the lights they had just plugged in popped, their bulbs exploding outward. This sudden noise startled all three of them, especially Bill who was standing closest to one of the lights.

Then they heard something, a strange noise coming from the distance. With the noise came a bluish light, then more orangey, and now green. This light, along with the noise, was coming from outside the house.

Like zombies from a bad movie, they all started moving in slow motion, ambling towards the large patio door leading to the beach. They held hands, bound together to face what waited for them outside.

Once through the doorway, they all looked up to the sky, walking still farther.

Streaks of solid colors, bisected by rivers of multiple colors, and muted wispy clouds undulated like waves toward them in the sky. The colors moved in concert with a strange whooshing sound, like a breeze.

It then occurred to all of them that the lights might never turn on again. As Max had told them all in his letter, this *was* the worst-case scenario. The sun would forever send massive electro-magnetic pulses into the atmosphere, generation after generation, rendering all electronics useless.

This *was* the new normal.

They would forever reside in a new Stone Age.

43.

July 5th, 1860
Denver City, Sanatorium

Russell Thompson reached over and opened up the drawer of the wood table beside his bed. With his bandaged left hand, he pulled out a leather-bound notebook given to him by his mother years ago. With his uninjured right hand, he loosened the leather binding ties and opened the book for only the third time. He glanced at the first page's inscription, *The adventures of Russell P. Thompson III.* His deceased mother had written this in careful script. He beamed at the memory of his mother giving him this book when he was a teenager, after he had announced that he was going to travel the world as an explorer. His father never tempted his desires, calling them "fodder for idlers." His mother rejoiced in his ambitious desires of travel, adventure, and prospecting.

Past a page of writing, on the next was a drawing of a cicada. He had drawn it a week ago, meticulously studying and copying in pen one of the millions of those flying around him. It was a sign of his rebirth. A cicada first comes out of the ground every decade or so before being able to fly. Similarly, his crushed body had come out of over ten months of therapy. He was in his larvae state before coming out of his hospital bed, reborn. Now he was ready to take flight.

He turned back to the second page again to see his nearly illegible scrawl from the first time he cracked open the journal. It was titled, "The road paved with gold," followed by the carefully written block letters: GSV EVRM LU TLOW SRWWVM

FMWVI Z XLOOVXGRLM LU KROVW ILXPH, DSRXS SZW ML VZIGSOB KOZXV YVRMT GSVIV, RM GSV HGIVZN YVW, 143 KZXVH WFV HLFGS LU GSV YRT OLZM KRMV LM GLK LU GSV SROO ZH HVVM UILN GSV XSVIIB XIVVP XZNK. Below this, he had written in the same careful block letters, USE ATBASH.

He didn't need to study the letters using the Atbash cipher he had used to write those words from the tip. The words were already committed to his permanent memory: "The vein of gold hidden under a collection of piled rocks, which had no earthly place being there, in the stream bed, 143 paces due south of the big lone pine on top of the hill as seen from the Cherry Creek Camp."

It was a reminder of his unfinished purpose. He turned the page, past the drawing, this time forcefully, and with his good right hand he started to write:

5 July, 1860

I can no more explain how I am alive, than I can waking up in this Denver City sanatorium bed, the very same bed of a dying man who gave me my very reason for coming to Colorado, seemingly a lifetime ago. I should be dead. This I know for certain. There is no logical reason for my survival. Yet here am I, convalescing from burns which I fear will forever remind me of that event, barely ten months previous. I remember feeling the heat and the pain and then blackness. After waking up a fortnight later, my attendants told me what had transpired. I was one of a multitude who were injured that morning. Many perished, perhaps even my friend Pete who accompanied me on this trip. I am certain he was more than a vision from that faithful day. I had thought destiny had turned against me as some sort of punishment.

He paused in his writing, looking to his left leg, which, along with his left arm, had been totally burned and broken, but was now mostly healed. Both arm and leg tingled together, an endless chorus of painful noise sung loudly from each. More painful was the knowledge that his father was the one paying for his treatments. The physical and emotional pain had been, until today, held back by the laudanum. He no longer wanted to cloud his thinking with the tincture of opium, so ignoring the clarion call of pain, he turned his back on his injuries and continued his thoughts:

Destiny has a curious way changing one's course. Only yesterday, I learned I was in the same bed as had been the lunger who told me his story in my hometown of Lawrence and gave me the tip that would lead me to gold. Because of his TB, he sought medical aid from this sanatorium, one that received worldly acclaim.

Betty, a beautiful angel, working as an attendant, nursed me back to health over these many months on a daily course of the sundry tales and life stories of the sanatorium's patients. Listening to her stories, witnessing her kindness, and beholding her beauty, an unspoken love had welled up in me, suppressed until yesterday, by the fear I would never possess the will to express my feelings for her. Then I learned the truth about my painful calling.

After returning from my regular walk, exorcising the demons of agony possessing my leg, Betty told me of one patient in particular. *He was in the later stages of TB,* she said tearfully. *In one of his bouts of delirium, he said that he had struck it rich, uncovering the gold find of the century. All he had to do was get back to Kansas City to get help and lay claim to his find.* She feared that he never made it back. I don't know why, but I never let on that I was bound to this same man and that I alone possessed his most cherished secret before he later died.

One cannot claim this as luck, any more than one can claim a new sunrise or sunset as accident. After all, what are the chances of one randomly finding a stranger with a secret that will change one's life, then surviving the oddest of events I dare say ever witnessed by man, and then falling in love with one's attendant, and waking up in the same bed as that stranger? Pondering such wonders makes my head hurt. The how perhaps will never be known, but the why is certain. It is still my destiny and purpose to find this gold and then propose to the woman I love. I will not be dissuaded from either of my missions.

He closed the book, and then wrapped it in a leather hide, folding each corner carefully, finally securing the hide to the book with a long leather strip, which was tied around its width and length.

~~~

Betty was looking forward to seeing Russell. He was nothing to look at, and was a little bit of a dreamer, but something had changed since yesterday. It was as if he had awoken from a dream, and he was alive again. She was excited to see what he would be like today. All night, until she arrived for her shift, she was filled with happiness. She could not wait to see him, and she hoped he felt the same.

She spent extra time getting her makeup just right, adding an extra measure of red to her lips and color to her checks. She brushed her thick black hair for longer than normal. She pressed her uniform, making it look crisp and nearly new. She wanted to look perfect for Russell, and hoped and prayed he would notice.

After visiting Mr. Jenkins, she entered Russell's room. He wasn't there. His bed, the second of eight separated by curtains, was turned down and his belongings were apparently gone as well. She walked up and saw there was a letter on his pillow that bore her first name. She opened it and read:

Dearest Betty,

You have saved me not only from my physical ailments but also from those much more disabling in my mind. I have a new sense of purpose that I have never felt until now. I have also fallen in love with you. I know that I will not be able to ask you for your hand until I have made something of myself. So, I will take leave for a short while. Know this, my love, although I am leaving you now, I promise to return for you. I can only hope that you feel for me the same love I feel for you. If, however, you do not, I am still joyous that you have given me so much to hope for. I pray that that day when I am able return to you will come swiftly.

Until then, I remain ever yours,

Russell P. Thompson III

44.

Revelation
"A Time Long Ago..."

Gord had tried to walk only during the night, something they were all taught, avoiding the daytime and its ruinous light. However, the journey was so long he feared he would never reach his destination. He kept his walking during daylight to a minimum, knowing the risks, and had actually only started in the last lunar cycle. He covered much more territory when he found the ancient trails made by previous masses of people. Some of these trails were huge, at least thirty arm lengths wide, and it appeared that many of the trees had been removed to make traveling easier. Oddly, a small channel separated some of the widest spans, as if a mighty river, which had since dried up, once parted the middle of these clearings. He would have enjoyed seeing what these trails looked like when they were built--and maybe even seeing their builders.

Every so often, one of these spans would be blocked by an odd arrangement of large gray boulders, some standing tall like monumental trees of gray smooth rock. Often, these rocky arrangements were impassible and required that he find a path around them. When he came upon them, he couldn't help but see some design to them as if the loose arrangement of boulders had actually been used for something he would never come to know. Occasionally, Gord would run across some sort of warning, obviously posted by a tribe many moons ago, as there sometimes appeared to be writing on a flat surface that had long since been removed by the harsh elements.

He was covering a lot of ground right now and felt as if he was very close. Perhaps in a couple of days, but not much longer, he would find what he was looking for: a place called Cicada.

~~~

He lost track of the days. So many days were the same: waking up, walking many trails, avoiding capture or death by the few other tribes or the occasional wanderer who was desperate and not part of a tribe. Always seeming to get closer to Cicada, but never getting close enough. He was tired and frustrated, but still hopeful.

Gord stopped for a moment of rest and a drink of water. The end of his waterskin, a new one he made only a few suns ago, was cool to his parched lips, cracked from the sun. He drank eagerly of the life-giving liquid, careful not to drink too fast. Wiping the wetness from his hairy cheeks and chin, he noticed the dirt from the path caked his hands and no doubt his face, as well. Looking down, he saw that his feet, wrapped in freshly cut skins, were also a gray-black color that matched the path beneath his feet. His legs were a matted mess of hair and dirt, all the same color. A nodule on his right knee marking where he had fallen shortly after sunrise seeped blood and pus, which had run down his leg, adding the only color to his person. Finishing the inspection, he examined his waist, then chest and then back out to his arms. He imagined he was a pretty scary looking figure right now. He smiled a smile he couldn't see.

He took in another swallow of water and only then realized something had changed. The air was different here. Normally, it was dusty, like it was now, and sometimes he would smell an animal or the unending yellowish-grey trees around him, but rarely did he smell anything else. Where he stood now, a new scent assaulted his senses, full of death and decay. He was close to people.

Immediately his mind was on alert and he knelt down, making himself smaller and less visible. This was something his father had taught him to do when he hunted or was being hunted. Gord searched all around himself to make sure no one was watching. He seemed to be the only one on a long hill, maybe 200 arm spans high, above a long valley.

Before him, the three-pointed mountain top he had been walking to for countless days was prominent overhead. These final steps had been aided by a flat surface on which he could easily walk. Again, another passageway used by masses of people.

He stood up for a moment. In the distance, not far but just far enough he couldn't clearly see, was what looked like a large marker in the middle of the path. Beyond the marker was a barrier twice his height, and above this was something he couldn't explain. The sky above the barrier seemed to reflect some of the sunlight back to him. This made no sense, as there was nothing in the sky to cause this reflection. He started walking toward this marker, first slowly, attempting to soften the noise of each footfall, so as to not alert another. As the distance between him and the object shrank, his pace quickened, as there was now an excitement in his step. It felt familiar, as if he had seen what was becoming clearer. The marker was like a large pile of stones, but smoother than normal and almost silver in color. Inset was a large, white, flat surface that reflected the blinding light of the afternoon's sun right back at him. He squinted and shielded his face with a hand, failing to blunt the harshness of the light that assaulted his vision, unable to see yet what lay upon that surface.

The *crunch – crunch – crunch* of his footfalls almost

marked a running pace. Abruptly, he stopped. Standing up straight to get a better look, he stared at the marker, which now stood before him. The cloud of dust churned up by and trailing his swift passage had now caught up and dispersed past where he stood.

He was motionless for a long breath, taking in what was now plainly visible. The marker was definitely older than he was. It must have been made by one of the great technology tribes his father's father, Stepha, had told him about; the examples of their existence he had witnessed many times during his long pilgrimage. The marker was as tall as he was and appeared to be made of a smooth reflective material. He remembered it being called "metal." Taking up almost half of the surface was a perfectly square placard of thin reflective material with a white finish, permanently mounted to the marker.

It had fancy writing on it with a drawing in the lower middle portion. Over the writing and the drawing, someone had roughly written something else, presumably later. It said:

The drawing was very familiar to him. When he was standing in front of it, he knew exactly where this image came from.

Gord removed a large cloth sling from his back, which contained all of his belongings. Placing it on the ground beside him, he pulled out a rectangular object and placed it in front of his feet, between the marker and him. He carefully untied a strap that bound the object. Then he unfolded the flaps of leather protecting the prized possession within. He picked up what was inside, what people before him had called a "book." Gord believed it was one of the only books left in all the lands.

He opened the cover. On the first page was written:

"The Adventures of Russell P. Thompson III"

On the third page was the drawing he remembered so well. He held the book and its drawing up to compare it to the image on the marker. It was the same.

He had found Cicada. He had reached his destination.

Before Gord could focus on his next step, an emaciated man, wearing dirty rags for clothes, stepped quietly behind Gord striking him with a large tree branch. Gord lost consciousness without seeing either the man or the tree branch before it struck.

The STONE AGE saga continues in

DESOLATION

The following chapter from DESOLATION is provided next as a bonus

10 days A.E.

"I know not with what weapons World War III will be fought, but World War IV will be fought with sticks and stones." ~ Albert Einstein

"Albert got it wrong – World War IV will be fought and won by those who found all the leftover guns." ~ Maxwell Thompson

Deadly Waters

Rocky Point, Mexico

A loud screeching cut through the raw morning air, rousing Bill and Lisa King from a fitful sleep of restless nightmares.

The uproar was one more in the endless list of sounds they had never heard before, which made up their life after the apocalypse. It wasn't the frightening death-throe-screams that followed distant gunshots across the town's estuaries, or the constant electrical buzz that filled the atmosphere all around them. This sound was a monstrous and powerful outcry immediately outside their beach home.

Bill sprang out of bed, a .45 in his hand, ready to bring death to some poor S.O.B. who was probably just hungry and looking for food.

"What is that?" he bellowed.

"Don't know, but it's close," Lisa shouted barely loud enough to be heard, flying to the window, scarcely touching the carpet.

Impossibly, the roar grew louder. Its deep, penetrating tones were undaunted by their walls and attempts to muffle the assault to their eardrums. It sounded like some angry mechanical leviathan, tearing at the sand and coral with its metal claws.

Standing at the window, Bill pried open the blinds, his jaw dropping farther with each inch revealed. The source of that racket was worse than the prehistoric monster he imagined.

"It's a cruise ship?" He blinked, transfixed in disbelief. His wife's eyes mirrored his distrust.

The dark behemoth was a passenger ship but no less terrifying than a T-rex might have been, made malicious by the green auroras illuminating its hull, as though it had been belched out of the depths to destroy them. It crept up onto their beach, slowly pushed by some invisible force, intent on burrowing a bloody trail to town.

The screeching persisted for what seemed an endless amount of time, until the beast ran out of inertia. The high incoming tide deposited it less than one hundred meters from their property.

When the dreadful noise ceased, the relative quiet made the constant thrumming sound of the wind-driven sand drubbing the home's windows and outside walls sound louder. The hulk lay unmoving, as if asleep, and they stood motionless for fear of waking it.

The light from tonight's auroras was bright and pulsating, outlining the massive vessel's form. Out of the water, it looked much taller, not listing as expected but sitting upright almost as if it were properly parked in the port five miles up the coast. Each spectral blast of green revealed more of the ship's evil presence. A fire on the port side, evidenced by blackened scarring, made it appear that the devil's own giant hand had reached out from the ship's bowels, leaving molten prints burned into its hide from the first row of balconies up to the silent chimney stacks. When the pulsating light ebbed, shadowing the ship in a momentary darkness, it almost looked like a normal cruise liner awaiting tourists that would never come. For a ship normally carrying a couple thousand crew and passengers in its belly, there were no signs of life.

"Where are all the people?" Lisa spoke his thoughts.

The Kings shuffled outside to get a better view,

unconcerned about sporting only their undergarments. There were others outside as well on their patios, even the Smiths whose house had burned down next door. All gazed at the silent giant.

Each pulse of the auroras manifested the ship's malevolence. The ship then seemed to take on a more ethereal profile, like a hologram that appeared to throb with each auroral pulsation or gust of wind. This was more than a reflection of aurora light off the ship... *It was conducting electricity.*

A scream startled them, tossed about in the wind's riptides. The shadow of a female form sprang from the void of a doorway, darting along the jogging track located near mid-ship. The shadow raced faster as if chased by something unseen. Another terror-fueled scream broke free from the winds. Their eyes followed her as she ran toward the bow of the ship and leaped, choosing death over whatever heinous sprits possessed the liner. When she hit the sand below, she came to rest in a small, dark heap. No more protests or screams.

"My God. She jumped," Lisa yelped, and galloped off toward the ship.

"Wait, Lisa!" Bill shouted. "Don't go on the beach!" His words couldn't stop her. Lisa was going to try to save that woman.

"Lisa, no! The ship . . . It's . . . you'll be electrocuted!" Bill shouted between each breath as he raced toward her, arms and legs pumping, fearing he wasn't going to reach her in time.

Another, different scream forced both their heads up, slowing their progress. A second cry of pain then accompanied the first: a hellish duet serenading the evil ship. They saw two others also attempting to assist the jumper. One appeared to be convulsing, yet fixed in his or her tracks, and the other simply fell over, dead.

Lisa froze, then Bill; now next to each other, both

paralyzed by fear.

"It's the ship! It's a natural conductor." He paused to take in several gulps of air. "It induces current from the CMEs hitting us, causing electrical discharges to the water and sand." He paused again. "My guess is anyone on moist sand will get a nasty jolt of electrical current. Anyone in the water . . . well, you just saw." Both Bill and Lisa quickly confirmed they were on dry sand and then looked back at the killing field ahead.

There were others on the beach, all much closer, but all standing still, unsure what to do next.

A bolt of blue-green lightning erupted from the hull and exploded forward, headed inland. Its bright tendrils opened up, reached out, and struck each person near it.

The Kings' own neuro-electrical currents discharged then. They fled the other way, for home, panic propelling them at an unnatural speed.

Find out what happens next...
Will Darla and Steve find each other again?
Will the King family reunite?
Will Max get free?
Just what is Cicada?
What connects three different time periods?
Not everyone will survive!

 # DESOLATION
Book #2 of the *Stone Age Series*

http://StoneAgeSeries.com/book2

FREE EBOOK

Max's Epoch
- A Stone Age Short

Get the exclusive novella about *Stone Age's* #1 character, Max Thompson

Sign up for *ML Banner's Apocalyptic Updates* (Readers list) and get a free copy of the exclusive novella (not available on Amazon or any other book sales channel), *Max's Epoch – A Stone Age Short.*

Just who is Maxwell "Max" Thompson? You know him as a prepper and close friend of the Kings, but why? What happened in Iraq? Who's bugging his phones? Who's after him? These questions and more are answered in the new exclusive *Stone Age Short.*

Click here for your copy: http://Mlbanner.com/free

Epilogue
A few words to my readers...
THE REAL STORY ABOUT CMEs

Stone Age presupposes what might happen if a series of massive, cascading CMEs or coronal mass ejections were to hit the Earth. How realistic is the story? Does science actually back up the plausibility of a large CME, and if so, is it possible that one large enough could destroy our technology and with it, our society?

Here is the really scary part: this very thing already happened in 1859. Yes, that 1859. The story of Russell Thompson is fictional, but the bombardment by two CMEs of our Earth is completely true. Miners in Colorado really started preparing their breakfast around 2 in the morning, believing the sun was rising. People in Cuba thought their sky was on fire due to the magenta hues of auroras never before seen that far south. Compasses worldwide ceased functioning. US and European telegraph lines were down for weeks. Some were electrocuted. And fires all over erupted, spawned from the electrical discharges caused by the CMEs.

Fluctuations in the sun's magnetic field trigger a portion of the sun's surface to expand rapidly, causing the ejection of particles into space. Most of these particles do not reach Earth; the few that do harmlessly interact and bounce off the Earth's magnetic field. Northern and southern lights offer testimony to the constant offensive of these particles. Very large CMEs, on the other hand, release billions of tons of particles, and when they hit, they disrupt and penetrate Earth's protective magnetic shield, called the magnetosphere. Because magnetic waves can induce electricity, it follows that massive CMEs, like those occurring in 1859, would induce large amounts of electrical current in any conductor on Earth.

What would happen then if solar super storms like those 150 years ago were to occur today? Our nation's power grid, already operating at or near capacity, is very vulnerable and would be easily overloaded by a large CME. A 2007 *Solar Storm Threat Analysis* report estimated that due to the lack of shielding protection, 250 million power line transformers and 6,000 major transformers would be destroyed by a major CME, similar to the one already seen in 1859. Our networked power grid would go down for a long time. Conceivably, it would take decades to rebuild. Consider what it would be like if just the city of New York lost all power for 10 years. The chaos and ensuing death would be unimaginable. Well, I'm sure you can better imagine it now.

The news gets worse. Now imagine all solid-state electronic circuitry in computers, phones, appliances, cars, etc. Those not protected, which is almost all of them, would be destroyed by the massive electrical currents created by a large enough CME. The Internet would be gone, along with all our massive worldwide knowledge base stored on electromagnetically sensitive hard drives. All of this together would cause the machinery of our economy and society to stop completely: all manufacturing, supply lines, transportation, communication, everything. Delivery of our most elemental necessities, such as food, water, and medicine, would be permanently disrupted.

Hardest hit would be urban areas. All supplies, not stored up but delivered as needed, would disappear quickly, leaving the population to fight for the remaining scraps. Leaving would be impossible. Where would you go on foot? Money would be worthless. The worst in human nature would rise to the top, as there would be little law enforcement without transportation to bring accountability to these areas.

Hundreds of millions would unquestionably die from disease, murder, and starvation. All societies fueled by technology would most definitely collapse. It is a bleak story, and it would most certainly happen if an 1859 event were to occur today.

What are our chances of something like this occurring? Fairly good, I'm afraid. Some scientists are currently predicting a 60% chance of this type of event occurring in the next 10 years. Yes, a 60% chance. Yet, as a society, we do nothing to protect ourselves from such an event.

Sounds dire, doesn't it? It could be even worse. Consider some scientists have argued that a mega-flare ten times greater in strength than the Carrington Flare hit Earth in A.D. 775. The proof is in the tree rings, with a spike in Carbon-14 readings that bears no other explanation.

I am admittedly someone obsessed with eschatological (i.e. end-of-the-world) theories/stories. However, when I read about the 1859 Carrington event, I was amazed at how underreported it was, until now. The *Stone Age* story is my way of bringing some light to an event far more likely (60%) than a global warming disaster (unknown %), or asteroid collision (smaller %), or even an alien invasion (0%). Yet, how much do we spend on the prevention or investigation of these? It is estimated that it would cost $200 million or more per year to start shielding the transformers that make up the power grid. This is a small price to pay, when you consider the cost of replacing it after The Event would run into the $ trillions and the lives of hundreds of millions, and surely the very lifestyle we take for granted every day could end permanently.

What is it worth to you to protect this?

Our technology is a house of cards, which if destroyed would take with it our complex and diverse society. Consider this the next time you turn on a light switch, adjust your air conditioner, drink your hot coffee, take a shower, drive your car, shop for freshly delivered food, answer your cell phone, search the Internet, withdraw money from an ATM, post on Facebook, and so on. All of this could be gone in an instant. The result would be catastrophic. Perhaps, we would see another Stone Age.

Thank you for reading,

M.L. Banner

Did you like STONE AGE?

Please leave a review
http://stoneageseries.com/book1

Reviews are vital to indie authors. If you liked this book, I would really appreciate your review.

Thank you!

Want to join in discussions about STONE AGE?
Positive or negative comments, it doesn't matter. Join the discussion here:

StoneAgeSeries.com/What-Are-Readers-Saying

Who is ML Banner?

Michael "ML" Banner is an award winning, international best-selling author of apocalyptic thrillers.

Three of his six published books were #1 Amazon best-sellers in one or more genres. Highway won the 2016 Readers Favorite Gold Medal in Thrillers and 2016 Finalist for Kindle Book Review's Best Sci-Fi Novel. His work is traditionally published and self-published.

A serial entrepreneur, having formed multiple of businesses over the years. He founded and still dabbles in SmallBiZ.com which helps small businesses form and maintain entities, forming almost 100,000 entities over its 17 years of existence.

When not running a business or writing his next book, you might find Michael hunting, traveling abroad, or reading a Kindle with his toes in the water (name of his publishing company) in the Sea of Cortez (Mexico). That's because he and his wife split time between their homes in Tucson and on a beach in Mexico.

Want more from M.L. Banner?

MLBanner.com

Receive FREE books &

Apocalyptic Updates - A monthly publication highlighting discounted books, cool science/discoveries, new releases, reviews, and more

Keep in Contact – *I would love to hear from you!*

Email: michael@mlbanner.com
Google+: google.com/plus/+mlbanner
Facebook: facebook.com/authormlbanner
Twitter: @ml_banner

Made in the USA
Columbia, SC
31 May 2017